MW01129829

# AN EMPEROR AMONG US

The eccentric life and benevolent reign of Norton I,
Emperor of the United States, as told by Mark Twain

—— DAVID ST. JOHN ——

iUniverse, Inc.
Bloomington

An Emperor Among Us
The eccentric life and benevolent reign of Norton I, Emperor
of the United States, as told by Mark Twain

iUniverse books may be ordered through booksellers or by contacting:

iUniverse
1663 Liberty Drive
Bloomington, IN 47403
www.iuniverse.com
1-800-Authors (1-800-288-4677)

ISBN: 978-1-4759-6104-1 (sc)
ISBN: 978-1-4759-6103-4 (hc)
ISBN: 978-1-4759-6102-7 (e)

Library of Congress Control Number: 2012921077

Printed in the United States of America

iUniverse rev. date: 11/19/2012

Dedicated to my best friend, my best critic,
my biggest fan, my *Anam Cara*,
my lover, my wife, Aurore

"I know who I am and who I may be, if I choose."

Miguel de Cervantes Saavedra
*Don Quixote*

•

"Have We An Emperor Among Us?"

The headline from the *California Bulletin* Newspaper
September 17, 1859

# CHAPTER 1

*The cigar smoke hung heavy in Mark Twain's sitting room. Large enough to accommodate all 20 members of the Monday Evening Club, it was not designed as a smoking room for such a large gathering. For a modicum of comfort, the windows were opened for ventilation, despite the cold winter air which wafted through the room, only partially abating the cloud of smoke.*

*The Monday Evening Club was a private club composed of invited members. Its purpose was to enjoy a fine dinner hosted by a member of the club followed by a presentation, or the reading of a paper by a fellow member of the club. This evening's gathering was hosted by Mr. Mark Twain, and featured a presentation by him as well. He, more than the others, liked the idea of killing two birds with one stone and meeting the two requirements concurrently.*

*Dinner having been finished, the members gathered in the sitting room, anxious to hear what Mr. Twain had to say. Once they were settled, the whiskey and brandy were poured. Mark Twain removed a cigar from the humidor, went to the front of the room, and stood before the large, crackling fireplace. He placed his glass of whiskey on the mantle, raised his hand, and waited for silence.*

"The Trouble Will Begin at Eight." That's the clever slogan I employed when advertising my lectures many years ago in Nevada and California. It worked very well, creating interest in my upcoming appearances. I have resurrected it for the publicity used to promote this evening's festivities: "An Invitation to the Members of the Monday Evening Club. Dinner and a Lecture at the home of Mr. Mark Twain, Hartford, Connecticut. Monday, February 2, 1880. Dinner will be served at six o'clock. The Trouble Will Begin at Eight".

Now, the dinner portion of this proposition has been completed, and it's time for "the trouble" to begin. So sit back, relax, and prepare to be impressed!

Being among friends, and fellow members of the Monday Evening Club, I certainly don't need an introduction. However, I am reminded of the time when I first began giving lectures back in those early days. For one of my early appearances in a place called Red Dog, a mining community near Dutch Flat, I was introduced thusly …

*"… Ladies and gentlemen, I shall not waste any unnecessary time in the introduction. I don't know anything about this man; at least I know only two things about him; one is that he has never been in the penitentiary, and another is that I can't imagine why not."*

While you laugh, permit me to pause a moment to light my cigar. You know, as an example to others, and not that I care for moderation, myself, it has always been my rule never to smoke when asleep and never to refrain when awake! So, bear with me …

I would like to make a departure from what I had planned to say to you tonight. It was going to be a reading of my paper on *The Decay of the Art of Lying*. I'm sure you would have enjoyed it, especially since I am an expert in that subject. But you'll have to wait to hear it – perhaps for my next presentation to this exemplary group.

Tonight, I'm going to tell you a story – a true story – and, as most of you already know, I like a good story well told. That is the reason I am sometimes forced to tell them myself.

# CHAPTER 2

I was shocked and saddened when I picked up the January 10th issue of the New York Times and learned that my old friend, Emperor Norton, had dropped dead on a San Francisco street two nights before. First, let me tell you the details of his death, and, in doing so, I'll give you a brief overview of this fascinating man.

Joshua Norton died on Thursday, January 8, at 8:15 in the evening, near the corner of California Street and Dupont (now known as Grant Avenue), across from old St. Mary's Cathedral. The cause, they say, was sanguineous apoplexy – a stroke. Minutes earlier, he had been lumbering along the wet sidewalk, carefully avoiding puddles as he went, having only a few blocks to go to reach his destination – the 8:30 p.m. lecture at the Academy of Sciences. Suddenly he lurched and fell, and ten minutes later he was dead.

Although nearly penniless – a pauper dependent on the

goodwill of others – he had proclaimed himself Emperor of the United States and had wandered the streets of San Francisco for 21 years. Had he been a mere mortal, his death would have gone by barely noticed. But as he was the Emperor, notices of his death, I am told, have received more ink and more space in newspapers across this country than any other death since the assassination of President Lincoln.

It was a moonless night, and the sky was dripping with an incessant rain. Although not particularly windy, occasional gusts of wind quickly grabbed ahold of his oversized bamboo umbrella, yanking him forward. The walking stick he held in his right hand was used not only for steadiness, but also as a brake to slow his forward motion as these small gusts showed themselves.

Suddenly, his steps halted as he froze for a moment. He moved a bit, froze again, and then pitched violently forward. The umbrella flew from his hands, skidding a distance along the street and his walking stick dropped and cracked as it hit the ground, bouncing into the gutter. He fell to the sidewalk, first to his knees, then to his side, and finally rolling to a prone position. His large beaver hat fell off his head and rolled along the wet pavement, into the gutter.

A gentleman, walking nearby, witnessed the old man's fall and came running to assist. He quickly saw that this was more than just a fall. The old man, whom he recognized, was convulsing, and his beard was covered with spittle. He hollered out to anyone who would hear, "Call for help! It's the Emperor! He's having an attack!" Other people gathered near, and a local policeman walking his beat responded by calling for a carriage to take the old man to the City Receiving Hospital.

The crowd had grown and the questions and theories had begun. "What happened? Is he alive? Who is it? Oh, my God! It's Emperor Norton!"

The Emperor was placed in a sitting posture with his back supported against the side of the building. One brave soul had removed his own coat and placed it behind the Emperor's head, and the group of onlookers huddled close so as to protect him as best they could from the wind and the rain.

Despite their best efforts, intentions and prayers, he died before the carriage arrived. It was the end of the reign of San Francisco's famous citizen, Emperor Norton I, the Emperor of the United States.

Of course, he wasn't an emperor. Joshua Norton had sailed into San Francisco Bay 31 years earlier, in 1849, at the age of 31, with $40,000 in his pocket. Within four years, he had increased his fortune to about a quarter million dollars. In another four years he was penniless. In a singular stroke of bad luck he had lost it all. He also appeared to lose his sanity and sense of reality – at least as far as his own person was concerned. He disappeared for a time, then reappeared – much the worse for wear, and still without funds – proclaiming himself to be the Emperor of the United States. For a short time, he even added the title, "Protector of Mexico", in deference to our southern neighbors. Norton spent the rest of his life wandering the streets of San Francisco, making and enforcing his proclamations, selling his own private currency, and looking out for the best interests of his adopted city.

From his youth, he suffered under the constant delusion that he was a displaced Bourbon prince. Convinced that he was of royal blood, he felt he deserved the respect that comes with it. Despite the fact that he was merely a common man – a Jewish merchant from South Africa – and despite the fact that he was truly a failure in business, the people of San Francisco generally entertained his notions and played along with his fantasy.

He had become a fixture in early San Francisco. From the day he sailed into the bay in the autumn of 1849, to the day he declared himself "Emperor of the United States" in 1859, until this cold, wet January evening in 1880, Joshua Norton's life was an important part of the life and growth of the city.

Although a pauper, the people of the city fawned over him. Bankers bowed to him. Politicians groveled. Business leaders gave him gifts. Later in his reign, even policemen saluted. He dined in some of the city's best restaurants for free. He always had complimentary seats at the theatre, and he travelled gratis on the railroads.

On the morning following his death, the headline in the *San Francisco Chronicle* said it all: "Le Roi Est Mort" – The King is Dead. It elaborated:

> *On the reeking pavement, in the darkness of a moonless night under the dripping rain, and surrounded by a hastily gathered crowd of wondering strangers, Norton I, by the grace of God, Emperor of the United States and Protector of Mexico, departed this life.*

His death was reported across the country. Newspapers in Seattle, Portland, Denver, Cincinnati, Cleveland, and New York devoted a great deal of space to his death.

A major newspaper in Ohio gave him one of the longest headlines ever. It read as follows:

> *LAID LOW: Emperor Norton Gives Up the Ghost and Surrenders His Scepter to the Man on the Pale Horse. The City by the Golden Gate Mourns Her Illustrious Dead. An Emperor Without Enemies, a King Without a Kingdom, Gone to Kingdom Come. Supported in Life by the Willing Tribute of a Free People, He Drops Dead at a Street Corner and Now Knows What Lies Beyond.*

I like the part about "a king without a kingdom gone to Kingdom Come". It also says he now knows what lies beyond. As for me, I would find it difficult to make up my mind which way to go, as each place has its advantages: Heaven for climate, and Hell for company!

People described Joshua Norton in many ways, using many adjectives: He was proud, polite, fair, congenial, intelligent, noble, and wise. He was a visionary and a statesman, and under his fictional rule, San Francisco experienced a renaissance of civility.

Emperor Norton's death comes, ironically, at a time when I have been writing my next book, and basing one of the characters on this very man.

Most of you know that for my last book, *The Adventures of Tom Sawyer*, I based the main character on a number of boys I knew when I was one among them back on the Mississippi River in Hannibal, Missouri. Some of you also know that I gave him his name in honor of another old friend in San Francisco – the firefighter and hero, Tom Sawyer. I knew Tom when I was a reporter for the *Daily Morning Call*. Today, by the grace of God, he is still healthy and currently holds the appointed position of Inspector in the San Francisco Custom House.

But not so for Emperor Norton. He's dead. However, he will live on in my memory, in the memories of the good people of San Francisco, and after tonight, in your memories, as well.

My new book, tentatively titled *The Adventures of Huckleberry Finn (Tom Sawyer's Comrade)*, is due for publication sometime within the next few years. It will feature a character, a grifter, known only as "The King". I have based him on Emperor Norton. He is not based on Norton's morality nor his generous spirit – as the character of the King is the antithesis of the Emperor's – but, rather, The King is based on the Emperor's dress and his demeanor.

So allow me to tell you about this fascinating man, whose society I enjoyed for a time, and whose life I have followed, with great interest, ever since.

# CHAPTER 3

In June, 1849, Joshua Norton caught the fever. It wasn't the kind of fever that raises your body temperature and gives you a cough and a sniffle. This fever inflames your body in another way. It speeds up your heartbeat and blinds your eyes to almost everything but the dazzling prospects of finding your fortune buried in the ground. Like many other men from all seven continents, Joshua Norton caught the gold fever.

This discovery of gold occurred at Sutter's Mill in the hills of California in January, 1848. It created an excitement that spread not like a wildfire, but more as a simmer turning to a boil. News traveled slowly in those days. By late 1848 it had reached the East Coast of America, and by 1849 it reached South America and Europe and even all the way to South Africa, which Joshua Norton called home.

Joshua's life in that faraway place was not a fulfilling one.

He did not have the happiest childhood, although his parents did their best to provide for their children. Joshua was born in London, in 1818, to Jewish parents. In 1820, when Joshua was only two, they answered a call to help the Jewish community in South Africa. They pulled up stakes and moved the family to Cape Town.

A major part of Joshua's unhappiness stemmed from his heart-felt, though unfounded, belief that he was actually a dispossessed Bourbon monarch from France, adopted by this well-meaning Jewish couple. Where it came from, no one knows, but this belief greatly affected his childhood in South Africa and it had a major impact upon his adult life in San Francisco.

Joshua was well loved by his parents. He was afforded a fairly good education, but one would have to consider him very much a self-educated individual. He developed a love for reading and studying. He spent many hours forgoing the activities of the other children in favor of a good history book, or one about science and invention. He had every reason to be grateful – and he was – but he was still haunted by the belief that he was a royal child under protection in this faraway corner of the world.

There was one other youthful influence that had a lasting effect on Joshua's life. One of the local characters in Cape Town during his childhood was a man named Isaac Moses whose antics delighted Joshua, and memories of whom would stay with him. Known as "Old Moses, the Moneychanger", he was a former soldier – a captain of the 60th Regiment. Moses had been an officer in the garrison. Even though long retired from service, he was still allowed to live in the barracks located in the Castle of Good Hope which was nestled on the beach at the base of Table Mountain. The castle, shaped like a five-pointed star, had been built in 1666 and was the oldest structure in all of South Africa.

Using the castle as his home base, Old Moses would parade up and down the Heerengracht (the "Gentlemen's Walk") in Cape Town, yelling, "Alles flaussen and homboggery!" – translated loosely as, "It's all meaningless". A town oddity, he was the butt of many jokes. He wore eccentric clothing; an old, faded army uniform, a camel hair cloak, a wide-brimmed hat, and a leather bag slung around his neck. He smoked from a long elaborately-carved Meerschaum pipe.

Old Moses had a soft spot for children, and Joshua often saw him grumpily moving down the street, shouting his message, only to suddenly smile and greet whatever young people he passed. Joshua would salute the old man, and was always delighted when the old, uniformed officer would salute him back. In spite of his usual cantankerous disposition, Old Moses commanded respect from the sentries at the gates of the castle barracks. Their practice was to present arms whenever he approached. If anyone failed to show proper respect, Moses would excoriate them. Joshua was impressed with the degree of affection and respect people had for the old man, and he never forgot it. This was probably the strongest and most enduring memory of his childhood.

For a number of years, as a young man, Joshua worked for his father in his general merchandise and ship's chandlery store in Cape Town. Later, he opened his own store in nearby Algoa Bay. Eventually, he was ready for a major change in his life. His business, *Joshua Norton & Company*, had failed within 18 months. His mother had already died, as had his two brothers – one from illness, the other by a fall from a horse. In 1848 his father died while on a trip back to England to find a rabbi for their synagogue in Cape Town. Ten days after his ship docked, he was dead, leaving Joshua, now alone in South Africa, with a $40,000 inheritance. At age 31, new dreams were forming in Joshua's mind, and when, in early 1849, he read accounts of the discovery of gold in California, he thought he knew where his future lay.

# CHAPTER 4

How in blazes was Joshua Norton going to proceed? He had never embarked on such a life-changing or challenging journey. He had never thought of himself as a particularly adventurous person, but what did he have to lose? His family was gone, and his life in Cape Town appeared to have no desirable future. So why not throw caution to the wind? Was he reluctant? Of course! But Joshua committed himself to making this long voyage to San Francisco. With a bit of fear and trepidation, he booked passage on a ship called the *Franzeska*, which was to become his "home" for three and a half months. You might have called him a mariner with misgivings. He embodied the description found in Richard Henry Dana's book, *Two Years Before the Mast*. In it, Dana wrote, "There is nothing so helpless and pitiable an object in the world as a landsman beginning a sailor's life". Joshua Norton had read the book in Cape Town while he waited for the *Franzeska* to arrive from Germany.

A few long weeks later, having departed Cape Town on August 15, 1849, he was aboard the *Franzeska*, sailing across the Southern Atlantic Ocean en-route to Rio de Janeiro. Faced with the reality of being at sea, he now knew what Dana meant about beginning a sailor's life.

It took Joshua a few days to get his sea legs and to come to grips with occasional bouts of seasickness. He and his fellow passengers endured cramped quarters lighted by poorly-trimmed oil lamps that emitted generous clouds of smoke. They dined on forgettable meals consisting of an endless variety of dried food. They endured occasional on-deck baths consisting of sea water dredged with a bucket and poured over the bathers. They put up with every kind of weather – storms, calms, heat, and cold.

In spite of all this there was, indeed, a great deal of monotony day after day. On a ship, it is easy to tire of the view in a couple of days and one quits looking. The same vast circle of heaving humps is spread around you all the time, with you in the center of it and never gaining an inch on the horizon. As a result, Joshua had lots of time to read, to think, and to dream of his future. His conversations with the skipper of the *Franzeska*, Captain Nicholas Deach, were some of his favorite times. Having sailed to California once before, in 1846, Captain Deach was able to describe the sites he saw and people he met there, much to Joshua's delight. They discussed Dana's book, which Joshua had read for a second time along the way. More current news was gleaned from crews of the few vessels they encountered in Rio, and later in Valparaiso, which were returning to Europe and the East Coast from stops in California.

There is really no way to know what is in a person's heart and mind as he is in that momentous place of making such a life-changing journey. What was Joshua thinking on those last days of his voyage as he got closer and closer to San Francisco? It was over a three-month trip – 101 days, to be exact – and all this time he was thinking and preparing and reading about this new place, California.

Having a bankroll of $40,000, he began thinking it would be foolhardy to risk life and limb hunting for gold along with the thousands of other souls greedily fighting for their share. Oh, that thought had crossed his mind, and for much of that time he had the fever. His eyes were nearly blinded by his wild dreams. After much thought, he realized he could make a very good living supplying those hapless dreamers with the tools they would need to seek their own fortunes. After all, he had a great deal of experience, and how could he fail now, in San Francisco, amidst the frenzied activity and excitement of the Gold Rush? Why not open a mercantile store selling provisions to others, and at the same time invest in some real estate in this epicenter city. It is from San Francisco that most of the gold-seekers would be launching their exploits.

The temptation had been great to run off and take his chances but reason had prevailed.

# CHAPTER 5

The *Franzeska* battled strong, blustery headwinds as she tacked her way up the California Coast. Under ash gray skies, she had pounded into the waves that seemed hell-bent on impeding her forward progress. Under the command of Captain Deach, this old ship from Hamburg, Germany, was in capable hands, and on the final day of the voyage the weather paled in comparison to some of the storms she had survived on the oceans of the world. This was not the heaviest weather Joshua and his fellow passengers aboard had experienced, but after all this time at sea they had pretty much had their fill of it.

Captain Deach sailed past his objective in order to take advantage of the northwest wind which would carry his ship into the Golden Gate. Although now sailing southeast with the wind, the sea was still rough and the *Franzeska* rocked as the indignant water boiled under her keel. The only passenger brave enough to be on deck was Joshua Norton.

"There's the entry to the bay, across the port bow," yelled the skipper from his post on the ship's bridge.

Craning his neck to see, and holding onto the rail for support, Joshua squinted as he tried to make it out in the distance. Finally giving up, he turned, carefully made his way across deck, and struggled up to the bridge to get out of the weather.

"Where is it?" asked Joshua. "It all looks the same. Where is the passage?"

"Funny you should ask that," said Captain Deach. "You're not the first to have a problem with it. Explorers from Vizcaino to Drake have sailed past here, in all kinds of weather, without ever realizing the Golden Gate was there, or that the great bay lay hidden inside. It wasn't discovered until 1769 during the expedition sent by King Charles III of Spain. Led by Gaspar de Portola, a Spanish hunting party, on horseback, discovered it from the inbound side. How is that for irony?"

"According to Mr. Dana, it was Drake who discovered the Golden Gate and the bay," said Joshua.

They were referring again, as they had many times, to the book, *Two Years Before the Mast,* by Richard Henry Dana, Jr. Dana had sailed to the Pacific Coast in 1835 and published his book in 1840. For intellectually curious travelers, like Norton, it served as the only guidebook to California.

"I'm afraid Mr. Dana had that one wrong," said the Captain. "Drake never knew it was there. What he discovered was a large, open bay about 30 miles up the coast from the Golden Gate."

"How, specifically, did those Spaniards find it?" asked Joshua.

"They were hunting red deer, which were here in abundance. You'll still see quite a few of them if you venture out a bit," said the Captain. "As the Spaniards rode over the headland of Point Reyes, they saw the bay off to the west. So, to my recollection, the credit goes to Sergeant Jose Francisco de Ortega (his name being coincidental). Prior to that, no one knew this great bay existed even though it sits in such close proximity to the port of Monterey.

"As I have told you before, Mr. Norton, my first voyage to this coast was just over two years ago. January of 1847, it was. I recall that about 450 souls lived here at that time. In fact, with its growth, the City of San Francisco is newly named. Last time I was here it was the Village of Yerba Buena."

"Good herb," said Joshua.

"That's right," said the Captain. "Yerba Buena is Spanish for 'good herb'."

"Mr. Dana said that it grows in abundance around the bay," said Joshua. "And it is said to be quite aromatic. In fact, the Spanish settlers here were known to brew tea with it."

"You know," continued Captain Deach. "It was believed that San Diego and Monterey were the only suitable harbors on the coast of California. Hell, they even thought California was an island until back in 1702 when a Jesuit missionary traveled across the Colorado River and realized it's all hooked together."

"So where is the Golden Gate?" asked Joshua.

"From here, about the only distinguishing landmark is that solitary group of redwood trees on the summit of that mountain," said the Captain. He pointed to a large green outline on the horizon which was now almost dead ahead. That's on the north side of the Golden Gate. Point Lobos is on the south side, where you can see all those large rocks. Lots of ships have ended up on the shoals there, mainly due to the fog. In a few hours we'll be approaching the harbor and it will all become clearer to you."

"And all this wind should be behind us," said Joshua Norton.

Eventually, they were met by two steam tenders. After determining the ship's identity, one tender hurried off to report in at Telegraph Hill so the brand new semaphore tower could signal to the people in the city the identity of the arriving ship. They then proceeded to the port to locate a suitable anchorage, since securing a place at the only wharf on the bay would be impossible. The other tender stayed to guide the *Franzeska* in through the Golden Gate.

By then, most of the passengers had congregated on deck to witness their arrival. Norton and the others marveled at the beautiful passage they were moving through, which was only about a mile wide at its narrowest point. At such close proximity to the shore, they delighted in their ability to clearly see several herds of deer running along the edge of the water on both sides of the Golden Gate. Soon, huts, tents, and a few small buildings appeared on the southern shore at the base of a mountain, and the expanse of San Francisco bay opened up in front of them.

The one thing they were not prepared to see was the forest of masts that littered the bay. The small tender had to guide them through the maze of over four hundred abandoned ships, barks, schooners, and brigs. They had all been left behind to rot by crewmen and officers who had been struck senseless by the gold fever.

"Good grief!" shouted one of the fellow passengers. "Just look at that. It's a maritime graveyard."

Joshua was saddened to see such a sight, and remembered the elegy written by Robert Scott – brother of Sir Walter – on the loss of his ship:

> *No more the geese shall cackle on the poop,*
> *No more the bagpipe through the orlop sound,*
> *No more the midshipmen, a jovial group,*
> *Shall toast the girls and push the bottle 'round.*
>
> *In death's dark road at anchor fast they stay,*
> *Till heaven's long signal shall in thunder roar,*
> *Then, starting up, all hands shall quick obey,*
> *Sheet home the topsail and with speed unmoor.*

Joshua Norton was shocked to see the results of their greed and impatience. If there had been any idea left in his mind of going up to the hills and compete with this crazy and careless mob, it was gone in an instant. San Francisco was going to be the source of his fortune. Even that was going to be difficult enough.

# CHAPTER 6

On November 23, 1849, The *Franzeska* sailed into San Francisco Bay. With hundreds of vessels arriving every day, it was no surprise that moorage space was non-existent. The *Franzeska* had to anchor out in the bay as did virtually every other arriving ship. The solitary wharf filled up quickly every day. The tender had guided Captain Deach to the edge of a congregation of ships straight off the central waterfront on the west and opposite a large island on the east. One of the men on the tender indicated a general area in which the captain should drop anchor.

There was a great deal of activity as other nearby ships were offloading their cargo onto other small tenders, and passengers onto very small rowboats.

Joshua Norton didn't feel that he was in any particular hurry although the thought of planting his feet on *terra firma* again was enticing. Having a good, solid meal of meat and vegetables would be just what the doctor ordered. The shortage of vegetables on the sea voyage caused a great deal of disease and discomfort. Joshua decided he could wait a little longer. What are a few more hours after all those days and weeks at sea?

He observed the activities of all those busy people aboard the *Franzeska* and other ships, many of whom were very much in a hurry to get off. Their behavior degraded to the point of rudeness and downright cruelty to their fellow passengers as they fought for space on the few small boats that came to fetch them. It was every man for himself. Forced friendships, from weeks of close quarters on the ship, suddenly turned into adversarial relationships. It was a me-first frenzy to get ashore. Joshua, however, reveled in the opportunity to survey the scene and get his bearings.

He stood there, taking in the sights of the small city to the west of where the ship languished on a slightly choppy bay. He marveled at the hills and mountains he could see behind the town and wondered how it could ever grow beyond a certain limit, as the hills seemed far too steep to ever support buildings and streets and all the accoutrements of a bustling city.

On the pier, he could see numerous piles of luggage from the various ships that had arrived that day. He was sure his trunk, which had been removed earlier, was somewhere among them. People were scurrying around everywhere. Ships' crews were offloading provisions, arriving passengers were identifying luggage and fighting for room to pick them out of the piles.

The crowded streets were lined with buildings, some more permanent than others. Those along the waterfront and up the slight hill toward the plaza were made of wood. As the buildings thinned out toward the south and west, they seemed to be made of canvas, held upright by tall poles. It appeared as though they had been made from masts and sails – perhaps supplied by those abandoned ships that filled the bay. Numerous other buildings were in various states of construction.

Strong winds blew through the gaps in the hills, blowing sand everywhere. Joshua could see large clouds of dust, and their remnants in the form of small drifts, lining the streets and hugging the buildings. The plaza was not visible, but the top of its flagpole stood above the structures which separated it from his view. Its American flag flapped in the errant gusts which survived the trip down from the hills.

Joshua looked around, taking in the 360-degree view. To the east, he saw what appeared to be numerous islands, notably one very large one that he would later learn was called Yerba Buena Island – the same name by which the city was called until it was changed to San Francisco in 1847. The islands were a delicious, verdant green, including the large one, which was blanketed all the way to its high summit. Beyond, lay the imposing, gray face of Monte Diablo. To the north were more islands, obscured by the countless masts of deserted ships and the gray-winged gulls fluttering among them. Above the masts, he could see mountains behind the marching green hills punctuated with large stands of redwood trees. To the southwest, beyond the outskirts of the small city, lay countless sand dunes and fields covered with flowering shrubs.

Later in the afternoon, things had slowed down to the point that Norton considered making his way over to the deck from which people were departing. As he approached the rail, a young man shouted to him from below, "There's room for one more person. Sir, are you ready to go?"

Norton looked around. Ever the gentleman, he wanted to make sure that all the ladies had been safely disembarked. He wouldn't think of going if there were still a lady remaining who would want to take that place. In fact, there had been very few lady passengers on this passage, and they had all been removed some time before this.

He replied, "Oh yes, thank you. My trunk has already been taken ashore, so I only have two small carpet bags. I will just fetch them quickly."

"Hop to it, sir, we are ready to go."

Norton hastened to the other side where he had left his bags.

Returning with them, he handed them down to a crewman who carried them down the ladder, dropping them into the small boat. Norton followed slowly, carefully, down the ladder and gingerly settled himself in the one remaining place in the rowboat.

They arrived at the pier, and the young man rowing the boat helped everyone off, then quickly tied it off and ran up to the crowd, approaching Joshua Norton from behind.

"Need help with your bags, sir? Excuse me, sir. Do you need help with your bags?"

The noise was incredible. Amidst the deafening activity and loud conversations on the wharf, the offer was not heard.

Louder. Closer.

"Sir, may I help you with your bags?"

"Are you talking to me, young man?" asked Joshua. "I am so sorry, I cannot even hear my own thoughts."

"Yes, sir! I understand," said the young man. "It's really chaotic here."

"Thank you, I could use a little help," said Joshua. "Very kind. But do you not have to row out for more passengers?"

"No, sir. This was my last trip for today." The young man now had the opportunity to, perhaps, earn some extra tip money from people thankful for his additional assistance.

"By the way, what shall I call you?"

"Peter, sir."

They spent some time searching for Joshua's trunk among the disorganized piles of luggage. Finding it, Peter took Joshua's large carpet bag in one hand and the end of the trunk with the other, dragging it behind as they walked off the pier. The racket of the seamen, the dock workers, and the construction of an adjacent wharf, receded into the background.

"Tell me, Peter, what is a bright young man like you doing carting other people's luggage on the docks?" asked Joshua.

"I just saw that you might be able to use some help," said Peter. "I arrived earlier in the week and found a little temporary employment here on the bay. I'm going to be looking for some permanent employment soon, since I decided I'm not going out to the gold fields as I had previously thought. The captain of my ship has given me some references."

"You are not going to the gold fields?" Joshua asked. "Why not?"

"Well, sir, I'm not the hardiest of individuals, as you can probably see. Even rowing that darned boat is a challenge for me."

Peter was, indeed, very healthy looking, but very slight. He was tall, approaching, if not surpassing, six feet in height, and was very thin.

"Admittedly, I have led a very protected life," he continued. "I'm a city boy, and I've spent my life either at school or in an office, so I'm not what you'd call the outdoors type. Now, having seen what it's like here in this city, if you can call it that, and from stories I've heard along the way, I decided that life out in the hills would be death for me."

"I think you are very wise," Joshua said.

"Yes, sir. I decided I'd give it a go here. I'm sure I can find a job of some sort that I would be good at. I'm a hard worker, and quite intelligent, if you don't mind my saying. Thanks to Captain Ruggles, I have some references to start with. We'll see what happens. I can always wait my turn to go back to Baltimore if necessary."

"Let me buy you a meal, Peter. I would love to talk some more, but I am famished. I could murder a good piece of meat right now," said Joshua.

"I beg your pardon, sir?"

"That is an expression. It just means that I greatly desire a good steak. After all these days at sea, I am ready for some real food."

"I know how that is, sir. I have been on the *Balance* for 174 days and I, too, could use some land fare."

"The *Balance*?" asked Joshua.

"Yes, sir. That's the ship I arrived on several days ago – from New York."

"Well, Peter, I guess I should welcome you to San Francisco, too, then. So you were also in on the big secret, eh?" He winked. "I say that with irony, because obviously it was not very well kept."

Joshua was talking about the secret of the discovery of gold in the California hills.

# CHAPTER 7

Joshua and Peter had been two of those dreamers who came to California for the gold. Now, however, their dreams were tempered with a good dose of reality and the realization that they were destined for another path to success.

"Pardon my asking sir, but where are you from?" asked Peter. "I can tell by your accent that you're not from America."

"You are correct, young man," said Joshua. "I am from Algoa Bay."

His answer was met with silence and a quizzical look.

"That is near Cape Town. South Africa," Joshua said, clarifying his answer.

"Oh, yes sir. I know where that is. Among other endeavors, I worked for a time as a shipping clerk in Baltimore and learned a great deal about the major ports of the world," said Peter.

"By the way, forgive me for not introducing myself earlier. I am Joshua Norton," said Joshua, extending his free hand.

"I'm Peter Robertson."

To Joshua, Peter appeared to be in his late teens or early twenties. He was, indeed, tall and thin, but, in spite of his professed frailty, appeared to be quite strong and healthy. Peter's long, dark hair framed a face with strong features, and no facial hair. He exuded a great deal of youthful confidence.

"Nice to meet you," said Joshua. "Let us put an end to this 'Sir' business. Since we are going to be dinner partners, and, hopefully, friends, you can just call me Joshua."

"That sounds good to me, Joshua."

"Much better. Where shall we go for a hearty meal?"

"There's a good place just up here," said Peter. It's just on the south side of Portsmouth Square." He indicated up the small hill straight ahead of them.

They arrived at a saloon called "The Verandah". They stepped into the dark interior and indicated to the bartender that they wanted a meal.

"You want a perpendicular?" asked the bartender.

A what, sir?" asked Joshua.

"A perpendicular."

"What, may I ask, is that?" asked Joshua.

"It's when you eat standing at the bar."

Joshua and Peter looked at each other and shrugged.

"No," answered Joshua, "I think we would rather sit. Would that be called a 'parallel'?"

They both laughed, but the straight-faced bartender pointed to a table near the far end of the bar. Joshua and Peter were still chuckling as they made their way to the table.

"I think we may have to learn a whole new vocabulary in this town," said Peter.

Both men ordered steaks well done, with heaps of potatoes on the side. Peter washed his dinner down with a large glass of beer. Joshua opted for cider, instead.

"It'll be good to get our strength back with some good landlubber's grub," said Peter.

*"Upon what meat doth this our Caesar feed, that he is grown so great?"* Joshua said.

"That's Cassius in *Julius Caesar!*" said Peter.

"Right you are, my bright young friend," said Joshua. "I can see we are going to get along very well!"

"Chalk it up to a good Catholic education back home in Baltimore."

"Ah, yes, there is nothing as valuable as a good education," said Joshua.

"That's right," said Peter. "Four years at St. Alphonsus Ligouri School put me in good stead. How about you?"

"Oh, my goodness, mine was a hodgepodge of an education. Primary school at Grubb's Academy. It was an academy in name only, however, as Mr. Grubb was quite unconventional – although it would be difficult to determine what was conventional since he was the only schoolmaster in the area. He was a pinchpenny, never even supplying us with pencils and paper. We had to write our exercises using our fingers in boxes of sand. Easy to erase, too, don't you know!"

Joshua continued, "Mr. Grubb was Church of England, so we began every day listening to a reading from the Authorized Version of the Bible, and reciting a prayer from the *Book of Common Prayer*. Then, after school, I would go home to my Jewish house and would have to listen to my father chanting his prayers in Hebrew – a language I never learned, or wanted to learn, for that matter. Of course, there I was, a young Bourbon, a member of royalty, given to this family and sent with them to South Africa to save my life from assassins."

"Really!" said Peter, in disbelief.

"Oh, yes, that is a long story, but needless to say I was certainly out of my element."

"So I am friends with royalty?" asked Peter, trying to lighten the conversation.

"Yes, that is actually the case," said Joshua. "But do not make too much of it. Let us not allow it to get in the way of our friendship or our professional endeavors."

"But what are you? A prince? A king? An Emperor? I think I'll call you 'Emperor Norton'. Yes. That sounds good. Right this way, sir," Peter joked, pretending to usher in a gentleman. "The Emp will see you now."

"Let us not make light of it, Peter, this is really nothing to joke about." Joshua's irritation was showing.

Peter could see that Joshua was getting annoyed, so he graciously allowed the subject to quickly slide into obscurity.

"Tell me about yourself, and about your family," said Joshua, moving the subject away from himself.

"Name: Peter Donald Robertson," he said, as though beginning to recite his curriculum vitae. "Born July 14, 1827 in Baltimore, Maryland, home state of Francis Scott Key who wrote the "Star Spangled Banner". Parents: William and Sarah Robertson. Father immigrated from Scotland. He is a successful banker in Baltimore. Raised Catholic. Educated at St. Alphonsus Ligouri. Good marks scholastically. Bad marks in the nuns' book of behavior.

Joshua chuckled.

"One sister, younger, named Mary Brigitte. She's 16. I worked for a time as a shipping clerk in Baltimore Harbor, thanks to assistance from one of my father's associates. Found I didn't care too much for that line of work, and, hearing about 'golden' opportunities in California, decided to give it a try. Father reluctantly supported my decision, and helped with the $150 fare to get here. Mother cried for weeks prior to my departure, and most likely for weeks after. Sister neutral on the subject, but I'm sure she misses me."

A slight watering of the eyes gave away his true feelings. There was no doubt he missed his family. Joshua was amused and touched by Peter's statements, and felt a tug of sadness within himself as he realized, once again, that he had no one back home who loved him – that he had no one back home to miss.

Over dinner the two newcomers shared stories of their respective voyages to San Francisco, and quickly cemented their friendship.

"You said, earlier, that you were on the *Balance* for 174 days from New York," said Joshua. "Why so long? We only took 101 days total out of Cape Town."

"I think the distance is a bit farther," answered Peter. "But we did make a number of stops along the way, and we were greatly delayed in Talhuaco. Captain Ruggles had some major problems there with paperwork and legal documents. I think those local authorities were swindlers, trying to get some money out of the shipping line. Well, at least we are here at our destination enjoying this wonderful meal."

"You know, Peter," said Joshua, launching into one of his anecdotes. "It is with thanks to Christopher Columbus that we are enjoying these delicious potatoes with our steak. It is because of him that trade routes developed allowing various crops to be grown in parts of the world other than where they started."

He continued, "These potatoes, for example, originated in Peru, in South America. After Columbus discovered the way to the West Indies and the Americas, Spanish explorers came over and colonized South America and fell in love with potatoes, finding them easy to grow and nutritious to eat. They sent them back to Spain where potato crops thrived, and then on they went up to the rest of Europe, England, Ireland, and then over to America. Prior to Columbus, they never existed in these areas."

"That seems the long way 'round," said Peter. "Why couldn't they have come straight up from South America like we did?"

"They had not yet traveled up this way, let alone developed trade routes. That came later. But I will tell you what did come here directly from other parts of the world – rats! I have already seen a few – just on our walk up here from the wharf – and I know we will be seeing a lot more as we go along. There were rats on the *Franzeska*, and rats on the *Balance*, and there were rats of every description, I am sure, on all those abandoned ships in the bay. They are all newcomers, just like us!"

Joshua took a great liking to Peter. In spite of his relative youth, he had a keen mind and was motivated to create a successful life for himself. Peter didn't know exactly what he wanted to do in San Francisco, but if the right opportunity came along, he even had a small amount of money to invest in the business. The two agreed to discuss these possibilities in the coming days. In the meantime, they both needed a good night's sleep on *terra firma*.

"I've already secured a small room at the William Tell House. It's not far, and I'll bet they still have some vacancy," said Peter. "You can get settled there for the night and decide later on what you want to do."

Joshua liked the idea.

The William Tell House did have a simple room available and Joshua checked in, signing the register rather optimistically as "Joshua Norton, International Merchant".

Joshua found his room in back. It was actually more of a space than a room. Separated from the other spaces by large canvas sheets, it provided only a modicum of privacy. At least it had a bed.

It was the first night in three and a half months that Joshua could not lie there and hear the waves lapping against the bulkheads. He couldn't hear the creaking of the decks. He couldn't smell the smoke lingering after the ship's lamps had been extinguished. He couldn't hear the shrouds slapping against the masts. He couldn't feel the rocking of the ship under his bed.

It was the first night in three and a half months that Joshua Norton couldn't sleep.

# CHAPTER 8

On the morning of November 25, 1849, Joshua and Peter began in earnest familiarizing themselves with the small City of San Francisco. They had allowed a day to rest and get their bearings. Navigating on dry land seemed like a new experience. Now, time was afoot and so were they.

In 1849, the City of San Francisco was barely more than a village. There was a preponderance of temporary and makeshift construction – tents and shanties – primarily due to the nature of the nomadic population, made up mostly of men, who were always ready to move on to fairer fields, or wherever they thought their opportunities lay. Shacks and tents were common. The only buildings having any pretension to size or solidity were the hotels, gambling houses, and restaurants.

Portsmouth Square, the social center of town, was a head-spinning kaleidoscope of activity. To Joshua, it seemed like the entire world had collapsed and concentrated its mass of humanity in this one little spot. Every race, every color, and every custom seemed to be displayed in all the frantic activities taking place. There were people from every country of South America in varying shades of the same swarthy complexion. They wore all varieties of colorful cloaks and serapes. There were Germans, French, Italians, and Russians in sables and furs. There were Turks in turbans. There were pig-tailed Chinese, dark Malays, tattooed New Zealanders, half-naked Indians, and Islanders from the Sandwich Islands and the South Pacific. Beyond this were rough, crude, dust-covered Americans from every state. There were so many others that neither Joshua nor Peter could even hazard a guess as to their origins.

In addition to the sights were the sounds. Every step passed a new couple or group of people speaking loudly in unknown languages which, altogether, created a cacophony of sound unlike anything the two men had ever heard. From the hotels, stores, and offices on one side of the plaza, to the gambling houses and saloons which filled the borders on the other sides, streams of humanity went about their business like swarms of bees working in their hives.

Another unusual sight Joshua and Peter came upon were two seemingly endless lines of humanity originating at the post office on the corner of Pike and Clay Streets. One line extended down Clay Street as far as the plaza at Portsmouth Square. The other ran along Pike Street and crossed Sacramento Street, continuing farther than the eye could see. It was, as they discovered, Steamer Day, a monthly occurrence when the steamer would arrive with provisions, equipment, supplies and, most excitingly, newspapers and mail from the East Coast. Of course, this was the day the locals had to have their missives prepared and ready to be dispatched to families and friends back home.

Many of the people in line were tired, cold, wet, and miserable men, desperate to hear from their wives and families whom they left behind as they came to this faraway place in search of their future. Most of these men came to the post office the day before in order to obtain a desirable place in line. A large number of people in these lines were paid substitutes, earning their living by representing some of the more successful men, who would show up as their surrogates approached the doors of the post office.

Joshua noticed, as they paused to observe this scene, the stark contrast among different people according to their present reality. Those who were almost to their goal of entering the building were giddy and joyous, looking forward to getting their mail. The lucky ones who did, indeed, receive letters, would whoop, holler and dance their way out the door, barely pausing before ripping open the envelopes – with tears often betraying their delight. Then there were the many who came out empty handed, having been told that there was nothing for them. Some of these poor souls wept openly, having waited months with no word. Others with glazed eyes, stoic expressions, and tightly pursed lips, held back such obvious displays of sadness.

Both Joshua and Peter were deeply touched by what they saw.

"Maybe next time," Joshua thought to himself. "As for me, poor orphan prince that I am, that is one hurt I won't have to endure."

"Maybe next time," Peter thought to himself. "Is that going to be me a few months from now?"

The most disconcerting feature of the city was the condition of the streets. They were uneven and covered with a great deal of sand, blown from the nearby dunes which lay to either side of the city. Very few streets were planked. In the winter, the majority of streets turned into knee-deep mud and the filthy puddles multiplied. It became the norm for these puddles and holes to be filled with whatever was available – old bags of coffee, cases of tobacco, and barrels filled with spoiled provisions – as well as old discarded tools and equipment. Additionally, people were in the habit of dumping trash wherever it was convenient. This, along with much of the materials used for "street repair", was a welcome environment for the growing population of rats that now called San Francisco home. Avoiding rats during the day was challenge enough, but it was common knowledge that anyone walking at night had to carry a lantern and had to step carefully so as to avoid stepping on the very large rats which came out in abundance.

Before long, these muddy, trashy streets would slowly be replaced with planked roadways and sidewalks – and even later, they would be paved. But for now, they presented a filthy, difficult challenge for anyone navigating through the city.

During the winter of 1849, San Francisco suffered from disastrously heavy rains. At times the streets became impassable. Due to a lack of storage space, provisions piled high along the streets were washed away, creating even more hazards. In some cases, horses became mired in the mud and were left to die.

This is the environment that greeted Joshua and Peter as they did their best to familiarize themselves with this new city. In spite of all the obstacles, they pressed on.

Over the course of the next several days, Joshua and Peter talked about their plans for the future and how they were going to pursue their goals. Peter liked Joshua's ideas. They included not only a mercantile business, but also a commodity business handling such things as coal, brick and flour. If they purchased in large amounts – coal by the ton, brick by the thousands, and flour by the hundreds of sacks – they could buy at very reasonable prices and then resell them in smaller quantities at much higher prices.

Joshua became more and more convinced that Peter would make an excellent partner, and Peter was beginning to see this as a real opportunity.

Joshua strongly admired Peter's attention to detail, his common sense, and his realistic view of business. What's more, Peter had some money to invest. While it wasn't the money that was important, what mattered most was that a partner with funds, who could easily invest, will not make his decisions based on money but, rather, on what is best for the business.

Privately, Joshua bought a few parcels of land, including lots on three of the four corners at the intersection of Sansome and Jackson Streets. He also purchased a few lots on Rincon Point – a wise move, as the value of those lots increased dramatically when the Pacific Mail Steamship Company built a passenger terminal and warehouse nearby.

Joshua and Peter had done their due diligence in looking for a location to open their new business and found a place they thought would be perfect for Joshua Norton & Company. Arrangements were made to meet the owner, a Mr. Lick.

Joshua and Peter arrived at the small adobe building which was right near the water on the corner of Montgomery and Jackson Streets. Due to slow going following a brief rainstorm, Joshua and Peter were just a couple minutes late. Mr. James Lick was there waiting for them. He pulled out his pocket watch and pursed his lips in disapproval.

"Glad you could make it, gentlemen. Time is money so let's get down to business."

Joshua apologized for their slight delay. Mr. Lick was polite, but his voice had a slight edge to it.

"So you fellows want to rent space in my little building do you? What are your plans?"

"Well, sir," said Joshua, "we are opening our own business, Joshua Norton & Company, General Merchants. We will be buying supplies and commodities in bulk as they come in by ship, and selling them to the miners and others who have need of such things."

"Not a bad idea," said Mr. Lick. "So you're going to give old Sam Brannan a run for his money, are you?"

Joshua and Peter looked at each other as if to ask whether or not the other knew who Sam Brannan was.

Joshua hazarded a statement. "We are not familiar with that name, sir."

James Lick snapped back, "I don't have the time or inclination to talk about him right now, but you'll hear of him soon enough. It's just that you will have a lot of competition."

"We are confident of our success," said Peter.

"I like your attitude, young man," replied James Lick.

Mr. Lick was starting to warm up just a bit. Joshua thought he didn't look much like a landlord, or like a man who in his two short years in San Francisco would own so much real estate (they had been told that he owned a great deal). Lick dressed much like a tramp, in old, ragged clothes, having only one filthy, stinking suit. He wore a full chinstrap beard which stretched like a large brush from ear to ear. Although a very wealthy man, he definitely marched to a different drummer. It was said that James Lick was born out of tune with the universe.

Joshua finally broached the subject. "How much are you charging for rent, Mr. Lick?"

"Well, you know, there's a store up on the plaza with only a fifteen-foot frontage that was rented for $3,000 per month. Another one, about a block away from that is going for almost $4,000 a month."

"Crikey!" said Joshua.

"Yes, it's an active market," said Mr. Lick. "Do you know that cigar store just up the street? You can barely turn around in that place, and it's going for $4,000 per month."

"Of course," said Joshua, "those are retail establishments, and close to the square. I would expect that they would command a dear price. We chose this location as foot traffic is not important, and we will be selling only to the trade."

"I understand," said Lick. "I have taken that into account. But this is a good, solid building, with close proximity to the harbor, so I have determined it's easily worth no less than $2,500 a month." He paused to let that sink in. "What kind of security can you provide?"

"Well, sir," said Joshua, "I realize you do not know us. Who does know anyone in this town? I can only tell you that we are serious about our business and I am prepared to pay several months in advance."

Joshua knew very well this was a seller's market. The rent was steep, but certainly not unreasonable. If he didn't take it, someone else certainly would.

"And a security deposit equal to one month's rent?" asked Mr. Lick.

"Absolutely. We can do that," said Joshua.

The business was done. A deal was made. It was then that James Lick's gruffness turned into a bit of pleasant sociability.

"Where are you fellows from?" asked Mr. Lick.

"I'm from Baltimore," said Peter. "Joshua is from Cape Town, South Africa."

They thought Mr. Lick would focus on the latter and be most interested in someone coming all the way from Cape Town.

He surprised them, though, saying, "Baltimore, eh? Good old Baltimore. I spent a lot of time there. I'm from Stumpstown, Pennsylvania. I spent my youth there working as a carpenter, but it's in Baltimore that I learned to make pianos."

"Do you make pianos here?" asked Joshua.

"No, I gave that up in favor of real estate. Now, that's the way to go. Real estate. Especially now, and especially here in San Francisco. I tried diggin' for gold for a few days (and I literally mean a few days), but quickly decided that it wasn't for me. It's real estate, I say!"

"That's part of our plan, too, sir," said Peter. "We both had ideas to hunt for gold, but now we think that commodities and real estate will be our fortune."

"Right you are, boys! And hard work, of course. I worked very hard before coming to San Francisco, making pianos in Argentina and Chile, and finally in Peru …"

"Peru!" Peter interrupted. "According to Joshua, that's where potatoes came from!"

Joshua nodded, with a smile.

"You are obviously a very successful man," said Peter.

"Yes, successful. That's for sure," said Mr. Lick. "But I've had a lot of good luck along the way. It's like what Thomas Jefferson once said: 'I'm a great believer in luck, and I find the harder I work, the more I have of it'."

"A self-made man," thought Joshua, out loud.

"Self-made, you bet! I worked hard to learn carpentry and piano making. I kept on going – never gave up – in spite of unstable politics in those countries. I was even taken as a political prisoner for a time by the Portuguese."

"God bless you, sir!" said Peter. "Did you escape?"

"Well, I'm here to tell you about it aren't I? You bet I did! And God had nothing to do with it."

Mr. Lick was an atheist. As a self-made man he had no room for any higher authority than his own wits.

"I outsmarted those Portuguese. They took me to Montevideo and I escaped. Travelled all the way to Buenos Aires on foot. Later, I took my piano business to Lima, Peru. It was a big success, and I was there for nearly ten years. Then I came here in early '48. I travelled as supercargo on the ship *Lady Adam*, and was responsible for the cargo of coffee, rough mahogany, and cowhide. I would have come earlier, but I had hired Mexican workers there – yes, there were a lot of Mexicans down in Peru – and they ran home to fight in the Mexican War. I was left with a ton of orders for pianos and had to finish them all myself. That's what I mean by hard work. It took me a year and a half, but I did it. A man of my word, I am. I'm self-made alright, but of equal importance, I'm a man of my word."

Enough talk. James Lick had almost used up his charm for the day. It was time to say goodbye.

Just as they were shaking hands and taking leave of James Lick – pending the signing of a lease – a small, vibrant man came through the door.

"Oh, Domingo!" said Mr. Lick, greeting him. "I'll be ready to go in a moment. But first, come here and meet my new tenants.

"This is Joshua Norton … and this is Peter Robertson.

Gentlemen, this is my friend, Domingo Ghirardelli. Domingo is a confectioner, and he makes the best chocolate I have ever tasted."

"You are always so kind," said Mr. Ghirardelli.

"Domingo is probably my only friend. Nobody else around here seems to like me. I had to coax him all the way up here from Peru. He had a small shop in Lima. When I came to San Francisco, I brought 600 pounds of his chocolate and sold it all in record time. I told Domingo he ought to come up here where the whole world seems to be converging and make his chocolate. I said he'd be wealthy in no time!"

"Yes, that is correct," said Mr. Ghirardelli. "I tried hunting for gold for a few months, up near Sonora and Jamestown – just like Jimmy did. But no, I realized my calling is making chocolate."

"Well, we all went through the gold fever for a time," said Joshua. "But then we came to our senses, did we not? By the way, did you know that chocolate originated in Central and South America, and then made its way to Europe and then to America? Much like potatoes!"

Joshua looked at Peter. Another smile.

"Yes, it is true," said Mr. Ghirardelli. "*Theobroma cacao*. That is where it all came from."

"So, are you Peruvian?" asked Peter.

"No, I am from Italy. I grew up in Rapallo and apprenticed with my father who was also a chocolatier. I had very good training. Thanks to Jimmy, I have this wonderful opportunity. So you wait and see. I will make the Ghirardelli Chocolate Company a big success!"

"I have no doubt," said Joshua.

# CHAPTER 9

The morning of January 5, 1850 was a cold one. It was not the foggy time of the year, but one wouldn't know it. The clouds seemed to meet the bay, and the drizzle made it difficult to see for much of a distance. Joshua Norton, bundled in a heavy coat could be seen wandering around down by the edge of the bay.

Suddenly, a large explosion ripped through the silence. BOOM!

"Bloody hell!" shouted Joshua, recoiling from the blast.

The charge had gone off inside the hull of an old brig near the shore. The water spewed into the air in a large curtain and shock waves circled out from the spot. The old hull sank into place next to another hull already resting on the bottom.

Not only was the skyline of the city changing as tents were being replaced by brick and mortar buildings of two, three, and four stories. The skyline of the bay, itself – made up of all those abandoned ships, barks, and schooners that had been collecting as the crews left them in favor of searching for gold – was changing, too.

These forsaken ships were thinning out, finding new lives of various sorts. Some were reclaimed or sold and were being sailed out of the bay to rejoin their sister ships in a useful life at sea. Others were being dismantled for their rare and valuable wood, among other useful materials, which were being used in the construction of those new buildings in the city. Yet others were being scuttled as fill for many of the waterfront lots along the edge of the bay.

The original, and best, of the ship scuttlers, Captain John Lawson, was at work when Joshua Norton came down to pursue his idea of procuring one of those old ship's hulls for use as a storage facility. As Joshua winced and squinted through the drizzle-filled air, he saw Captain Lawson appear slowly out of the mist, standing at the bow of a skiff, looking like George Washington crossing the Delaware. In contrast to the earlier explosion, an eerie silence hung over the scene. The only sound he heard was the banter of the men in the boat with Captain Lawson, and the splashing of their oars as they approached the shore.

Joshua got a better look at him as he came closer. All of a sudden, he looked less like George Washington and more like the pirate, Jean Lafitte. Captain Lawson was tall, lean, had a short, thick moustache, a short close-cropped beard adorning his chin, and heavy black hair extending below a wide bandana. He was extremely good looking, save for a rather large disfiguring scar on his left cheek.

Joshua waved, and used his hands like a megaphone to make sure he was heard. "You are doing a fine job of cleaning up the bay, Captain."

Lawson waited until he drew alongside the dock. "Well, thank you, sir. Doin' what one loves isn't so much a job as it is an adventure, don't you know?"

"I understand," said Joshua. "Allow me to introduce myself, I am Joshua Norton."

"You must already know who I am, having addressed me as Captain. Yes, sir, I am Captain John Lawson, at your service. My friends call me John, but you can call me Captain Lawson." He let out a big belly laugh and slapped Joshua on the shoulder, almost hard enough to knock him into the water.

Joshua steadied himself with his legs a bit farther apart, just in case this exuberant captain got carried away again. "What on earth got you into this business?" asked Joshua.

Captain Lawson replied, "It was totally by accident – or at least out of necessity. I bought a couple lots sight unseen. What do they say? *Caveat emptor* – buyer beware. Anyway, once I got there I found out that my two lots were covered by 35 feet of water! Dammit to hell, I was upset!

"It was too damn expensive and difficult to haul rock and dirt into the area to fill it in. I looked out over the bay and saw all those old ships just sitting there and got the idea that I could haul 'em and sink 'em so they would make real good fill. I found a number of strong, hearty fellows who were happy to work for five dollars a day and all they could drink, if you know what I mean. In no time we had my lots covered with old hulls, and by the time we finished I had people lining up and begging me to do the same for them.

"So now we get paid quite well to find the old ships, load 'em with ballast, tow 'em over to just the right spot, and BOOM down they go."

"So, how is business?" asked Joshua.

"Not bad," replied the Captain. "Lots of orders. Just a bit of a problem yesterday. We sank the old *Cordova* beautifully, but then found out it was on the wrong lot!"

"Oh, dear," said Joshua. "That will sink your business!"

"Very funny," said Captain Lawson. Not to be outdone, he added, "When the owner found out, he really exploded." Lawson released another hearty laugh. Joshua braced himself for another slap on the shoulder, which was not forthcoming. "Is there something I can do for you, Mr. Norton?"

"As a matter of fact, there is," said Joshua.

"What do you need?"

"Well, my partner and I are opening a new commodities business in a rather small building just up the street. I thought one of these old hulls would make for a good storage depot for many of our supplies and products. Do you know of a suitable one for that purpose? At a reasonable price?"

Captain Lawson thought for a moment, scratching his beard with one hand. "It so happens I do," said the captain. "Check out the *Genessee*. It doesn't have any rare or valuable wood, so it's not really worth the scrap. While its sailing days are over, it's certainly in good enough shape for a storage building. I think the owner would sell it for a song."

"I am not a very good singer," said Joshua. "So do you think he might just let me have it cheaply?"

"If you're a terrible singer," said the captain, "then just start singing and don't stop until he begs you to just take the damn thing!" Another deep belly laugh and another slap on the shoulder. This time Joshua was prepared.

Captain Lawson gave him the name of the owner of the *Genessee* and told him how to find the fellow. Joshua thanked him for his time and made a hasty exit before his shoulder got slapped again.

Joshua found the owner, bought the *Genessee* for cash, and arranged for Lawson to haul it and carefully sink it into place on one of his lots.

"I will be there to make sure you and your crew get it into the right place," Joshua had told the captain. "Be sure to do it gently. I need the ship in one piece if it is going to be useful for storage."

"I accept your caution," said Lawson. "After that earlier problem with the wrong location, we'll all feel better with your confirmation!"

The *Genessee* was sunk – in the right place, and in one piece

– and was eventually made land-bound with all the fill dirt surrounding it as the city expanded into what was once water. Joshua removed the masts and built a large wooden roof over the top to keep the contents dry. Surplus room on the ship was rented out to others for storage. It became quite valuable later on, during the time of the fires, as storage space was in short supply.

Joshua and Peter wasted no time getting their business set up and hanging their sign outside the doors of the office:

### JOSHUA NORTON & COMPANY
### GENERAL MERCHANTS

They began selling supplies for carpenters, miners, and seamen, as well as speculating in various commodities, including the flour, coal, and bricks they had discussed.

Profits were good. Very good.

# CHAPTER 10

With increased good fortune, Joshua eventually moved from the William Tell House to the four-story Jones Hotel. Providing nicer lodgings, the Jones Hotel was one of the newer buildings which had been pre-built and shipped in sections around the Horn from Baltimore. Joshua made sure that Peter was told of its noble origins!

Joshua and Peter were privileged to attend many cultural events. An increasing number of spectacles were brought to the City of San Francisco. Some were vocalists and musicians, and others were full-scale productions. Neither Joshua nor Peter were drinkers or gamblers. The boisterous barrooms, the chaotic gambling halls, and the dark and dirty brothels were all retrograde to their desires and interests. So these evenings out at the theatre were a welcome respite from long work days and lonely nights.

They saw the first-ever dramatic production in the city – a

play called *The Wife*, presented at Washington Hall. The general consensus was that, while a novelty, it was an utter failure.

The afternoon following their evening at the theatre, Joshua and Peter took a trip to try out the new ferry service across the bay to the "Contra Costa", as it was called – the "opposite coast".

It had been a typically foggy summer morning, but by mid-day the shroud had lifted and that massive tube of fog that marched in through the Golden Gate had vanished. After lunch, Joshua and Peter hopped aboard the steamer, *Kangaroo*, and enjoyed a few hours on the water.

Of course, this provided an opportunity for them to talk, which didn't happen much during their busy days running the business. The subject matter of the play they had seen the night before prompted Joshua to bring up the subject of marriage. As they stood on deck while skimming across the bay, he decided to broach the subject and asked Peter about his desire for finding a young woman with whom he could fall in love and with whom he could start a family of his own. Peter was certainly at marrying age.

"Is it not time an eligible young man like you started thinking about marriage?" asked Joshua, out of the blue.

"Gosh!" said Peter, falling back as though he were reeling from a blow. "You don't beat about the bush, do you? Haven't you heard of easing into a subject?"

"Why waste time on niceties," said Joshua.

"You're right. We know each other well enough by now to speak frankly," said Peter.

Joshua said nothing. He thought to himself that there was at least one subject he didn't like to speak frankly about – namely himself.

Finally, Peter spoke again. "I know you are asking in all sincerity, so I suppose you deserve a good answer."

"Peter, I did not mean to upset you," said Joshua. "I had been thinking about it. You are going on 23 years of age. By now you should be married."

"You're one to talk," said Peter, jabbing him. "What about you? You're past 30. Aren't you past your prime?"

"Sadly, yes," said Joshua. "I have let that opportunity pretty much go by. Anyway, I am a special case and have other matters to deal with. So do not worry about me. But you still have your life before you. You should be spending your evenings with a nice, young lady – not with the likes of me."

The *Kangaroo* rocked wildly after hitting a rogue wave. Peter and Joshua paused their conversation as they both grabbed ahold of the rail to steady themselves. Joshua sat down.

"I'm sorry I sounded so shocked. I just wasn't expecting it. Truth be told, it is a subject that has been plaguing my thoughts lately, so maybe I'm just a bit sensitive about it." Another wave rocked the boat. Peter paused and, after the boat's movement settled down, took a seat next to Joshua on the ship's raised cabin. "I've been looking," he continued, "but as you well know there aren't a great many women in this town. Of the ones that are here, the majority are of very loose morals, to put it mildly. You know what I mean."

Joshua cocked his head and raised an eyebrow.

Peter continued, "Of course you know what I mean. The whores outnumber any decent women a hundred to one. Of those women who don't work in the brothels, most are already married. I have no doubt that more women will be arriving as time goes on, but as yet, I guess I haven't been in the right place at the right time."

"How about those 'gold rush widows'?" Joshua was talking about the married women basically abandoned by their husbands who went off to hunt for gold.

"I know they have been abused by their absent husbands," said Peter, "but in fact they are still married to them. I'm not about to get tangled up in one of those situations. Hell, no! Don't think the temptation hasn't been strong. I am a healthy, young man after all."

"I realize that," said Joshua, and I knew that is what you would say."

"You bet!" said Peter. "Don't forget, you're dealing with a good Catholic boy. That's where my Catholic upbringing and religious education kick in. Just look!"

Peter held his hands out and made fists of them.

"Look at those knuckles. They still hurt from all the beatings they have received from the sticks the nuns carried around. Don't forget, I went to St. Alphonsus Ligouri School where I was taught – actually more like forced – to memorize many of the saint's writings. So when temptations do arise, to this day, I have been conditioned to automatically call to mind the 'Invocation of the Blessed Virgin in Time of Temptation'."

"You *are* a good Catholic boy," said Joshua.

"Well, Joshua," said Peter, "After an entire childhood of indoctrination in Catholic teachings, one hardly knows any different."

"How does it go?" Joshua asked. "Can you say it for me?"

"Are you absolutely sure you want to hear it?"

"Oh, yes. I, too, want to be prepared when tempted!" said Joshua. He laughed and gestured for Peter to stand up while he recited.

"Okay," said Peter. "Pay attention."

*Haste, my mother, run to help me;*
*Mother haste do not delay;*
*See from hell the envious serpent*
*Comes my troubling soul to slay.*

*Ah! His very look affrights me,*
*And his cruel rage I fear;*
*Whither fly, if he attacks me?*
*See, him, see him coming near!*

*Lo! I faint away with terror,*
*For if yet thou dost delay*

*He will dart at me his venom;*
*Then, alas! I am his prey.*

"It goes on from there. That's probably enough," Peter said.

"No!" Joshua protested. "Let me hear it all. You cannot leave a good poem unfinished."

Peter continued:

*Cries and tears have nought availed me,*
*Spite of all, I see him there;*
*Saints I can till I am weary,*
*Still he stands with threat'ning air.*

*Now his mighty jaws are open,*
*And his forked tongue I see;*
*Ah! He coils to spring upon me.*
*Mother! Hasten, make him flee.*

*Mary! Yes, the name of Mary*
*Strikes with dread my cruel foe,*
*Straight he flees, as from the sunbeam*
*Swiftly melts the winter's snow.*

*Now he's gone, but do thou ever*
*Stay beside me, Mother dear;*
*Then the hellish fiend to tempt me*
*Nevermore will venture near.*

"I like that," said Joshua. "It is important to have some form of strength to keep one on the straight and narrow, and if, for you, it is the Blessed Virgin Mary, then I say carry on!"

"My faith is important to me," said Peter. "I don't think I could survive this experience without it."

"It should be important to you. Sometimes I envy, if that is allowed, the certainty of your faith. As for me, I believe that all religious traditions have very important things to say to us. There is some truth in all of them. I find that it would be difficult to choose just one."

Even in San Francisco, as was his habit as an adult in Cape Town, and as he would for the rest of his life, Joshua often went to church, but rarely the same one twice in a row. He believed that they all had some good things to say, and he wanted to experience a well-rounded religious life. For Peter, needless to say, it was Mass every Sunday.

As time went on, they went to other plays and musical performances. Of note were concerts at the National Theatre by the renowned Viennese pianist Henri Herz, who played his own concertos. They saw the first grand opera presented in the city – Bellini's *La Sonnambula* at the Adelphi Theatre.

Another production. Another inspiration. Part of the story of *La Sonnambula* involves a young stranger named Rodolfo, who is ultimately identified as the long-lost heir of the local count. It was a beautiful love story, but it brought to the forefront of Peter's mind the statement that Joshua had made, quite seriously, about his being a long-lost heir of the throne of France.

It was after the opera, before going to their separate abodes, that Peter finally got up the nerve to ask about it.

"Joshua, there is something that has been haunting me for some time and now, as I know you much better, I feel compelled to ask about it."

"Uh oh. Are you going to ask me some personal questions now?"

"It has to do with something you said shortly after we first met. I haven't heard you mention it since then, but it has been in the back of my mind. It was brought to the forefront during the opera this evening by the situation of Count Rodolfo."

"Do not be bashful, Peter. It was you who criticized me about beating around the bush. I am a man. I can take it. So what is it that is bothering you so much?" Joshua furrowed his brow. He had a sense of what was coming.

"Well, you see, you talked about being a member of royalty – a French Bourbon prince, or some such, and that you …"

"Yes!" Joshua interrupted. "I can see how that might be confusing to you. What is someone like me doing in San Francisco working so hard and operating as such an upstanding and, let us say, normal, citizen?"

Peter could see Joshua taking on a whole new demeanor, one that implied a higher station, and that made him feel like Joshua was talking down to him, as a King might speak to one of his subjects. It wasn't what he said but, rather, how he said it. Peter also noticed a slight glazing of Joshua's eyes, as though he saw something that no one else could see.

"It is true, Peter." Joshua looked around to make sure he could not be overheard, and his voice lowered to a near whisper. "I am, indeed, a crown prince to the throne of France. My life was in danger, and, as a child, I was sent to be with this family who were heading for South Africa. They vowed to protect me, and to treat me as a member of their family."

"It seems as though they did a good job of that," said Peter.

"Yes, I suppose they did. The irony, though – one which always grated at me – was that this Jewish family named their own two children with proper Bourbon names: Louis and Philip; and I was given the name Joshua Abraham. How cruel is that?"

Joshua paused. He was revealing too much about his feelings.

"But they seemed to take good care of you," said Peter.

"Oh, yes. They provided me with all the necessities of life, but I was cheated out of the proper life of a monarch that was my due."

Okay, it was, indeed, getting too personal. Joshua looked intently into Peter's eyes. "In any event, you must not speak of this to anyone. They would think I'm crazy. Probably you do, anyway."

"No!" Peter said, not totally convinced. "It's just such a fantastic story."

"I hope this has solved the mystery for you," said Joshua, wanting to end the conversation. "It is not something you should concern yourself with. So, let us drop the subject and not speak of it again. We have far more pressing things to worry about, like keeping our business going."

And with that, the subject was dropped, though not forgotten.

# CHAPTER 11

Joshua was tired and covered with soot. Large rivulets of sweat ran down his face, and droplets spread down his beard. He had spent the last four hours working as part of a bucket brigade transferring water from San Francisco Bay up to the front line of the fire. The newly-constructed water reservoirs had run dry. This was a last ditch effort to stop the fire's advance. Joshua's hands were raw from handling bucket after bucket after heavy bucket of water, and he wished this were the first time he had had to help fight a fire. Unfortunately, he knew the drill quite well. The city was being threatened for the sixth time in a year and a half.

On this particular day, June 22, 1851, the fire had broken out early in the day in a frame house on the north side of Pacific Street near Powell. It destroyed the city hall and the Jenny Lind Theatre, and within these four hours had destroyed over ten complete blocks. The high winds – usual at this time of year – roared in from the ocean and fanned the flames into a fury. The fire jumped from street to street, and it was continuing almost unabated despite nearly everyone's best efforts. Desperate property owners fought against firemen in an attempt to prevent them from tearing down their buildings as a means of halting the fire's progress.

By the time the fire was stopped, late in the day, over $3,000,000 in damages had been done. It had traveled from Powell Street to Sansome Street, and from Clay to Broadway.

If life wasn't difficult enough, within the first year and a half, it was challenged for all of San Francisco by these six major fires that threatened life and property.

The first major fire occurred only a month following Joshua's arrival.

It was Christmas Eve, of all days. The fire destroyed much of the small city, consuming over fifty buildings. Starting at Dennison's Exchange, on the east side of Kearny Street, between Clay and Jackson Streets, it spread out and did $1,500,000 in damage.

As San Francisco did not yet have a fire department, citizens were organized to help pull down buildings with ropes in order to retard the fire. Joshua and Peter were among them, having spent all night helping to throw lines up to the brave men standing atop the buildings, securing the ropes and then jumping to the ground to help pull down the walls. Ultimately, the fire was stopped by blowing up a building with gunpowder – a relatively small sacrifice for the greater good.

The next day it was decided that San Francisco needed a fire department.

The second fire occurred only five months later, on May 4, 1850. This fire broke out at 4:00 a.m. in the United States Exchange – a gambling house and saloon. Ironically it had been built on the same site as Dennison's Exchange, where the first fire started. By 11:00 a.m., three large blocks of buildings were totally destroyed. This fire burned the entire block surrounded by Kearny, Clay, Montgomery, and Washington Streets. It then jumped over

Washington Street and burned across the plaza. This fire destroyed 300 buildings and did over $4,000,000 in damage. It was only stopped by the willingness to pull down walls and blow up many buildings with gunpowder. Many people, including Joshua and Peter, readily volunteered their assistance. Others flatly refused or would only consider doing so if they were paid for their services. Soon thereafter, an ordinance was passed requiring every available person to assist in fighting fires when called upon. Failure to do so resulted in fines ranging from $5 to $100. Joshua and Peter, along with the brave souls who fought shoulder to shoulder with them, had always felt the call to help. They would soon appreciate the additional manpower this ordinance created.

Unfortunately, the buildings constructed to replace those lost in the fire were flimsier, and bigger firetraps, than those they replaced.

The third fire was only a month and a half later, breaking out on June 14. It proved to be worse than the two previous fires put together. This fire started in the Sacramento Bakery, located at the rear of the Merchant's Hotel near the corner of Clay and Kearny Streets. High winds fanned the flames, and by the time it was stopped, it had destroyed another 300 buildings and burned all the way down to the bay. Damages were estimated at $5,000,000.

The next day, it was decided that San Francisco needed to provide a water supply for fighting fires.

The fourth fire came along on September 17, 1850. A hundred and fifty buildings were destroyed by this fire, which consumed the area bounded by Dupont, Montgomery, Washington and Pacific Streets. It broke out in the Philadelphia House on the north side of Jackson Street. Although it covered a large area, most of the buildings were built of wood and only one story in height. As a result, damage was proportionately low. Probably the smallest of the major fires, it did about $500,000 in damage. The affected area was covered with new buildings in a matter of a few weeks.

The newly-organized San Francisco, Empire, and Protection

Fire Companies had uniforms, but no water, to fight this fire. Despite the recognition, three months prior, of the need for a water supply, none had yet been provided.

Then, on May 4, 1851 – the anniversary of the second great fire – the fifth great fire, the biggest yet, almost destroyed the entire city. In less than ten hours, it had consumed 18 blocks and 2,000 buildings. About $12,000,000 damage was done.

By this time, many solid buildings, thought to be fire-proof, had been built. But when tested by this fire, it was found that the brick walls crumbled in the intense heat. Thick iron shutters, meant to block the fire, turned red hot and warped. People who had sought refuge inside these buildings found that the metal shutters and doors had expanded in the heat, trapping them inside these infernos.

A strong northwest wind blew the flames in one direction, and then, suddenly shifting, blew from the south, forcing the fire back in the opposite direction. The intense heat and expanse of the flames increased the winds, sucking in fresh air from outside the fire. The hollows beneath all the newly-planked streets acted as funnels which shot hot air into the flames, stirring them into even more furious destruction. The planked streets, themselves, turned into dry timber and succumbed to the flames, turning the entire area into fields of fire.

Water was available, and additional fire companies had been organized, but this fire was so big and moved so fast, they were challenged beyond their limits.

This fire also consumed a number of the ships that had been abandoned in 1849 and 1850, including the *Niantic*, the *General Harrison*, and the *Apollo* – which had been converted into a saloon.

Now, this sixth fire challenged the young city even more. If there is a silver lining to be found in these fires, one could say that they contributed greatly to the early maturity of this young city. They steeled the residents to organize, to build safer, sounder buildings, to plank and pave more of the streets, and to develop increasingly better methods of protecting them.

More permanent buildings – some quite beautiful – were constructed. Canvas tents and wooden shanties had finally disappeared from the center of town. In fact, by 1853, San Francisco was starting to look like a real city. By the end of that year, there were over 600 buildings constructed with stone or brick, many of which were three stories or higher.

With the previous fire, only seven weeks before, every major newspaper building had been destroyed, save for the *Alta California*. With this fire, oddly enough, all the others, which had been rebuilt, survived – while the *Alta California* had its turn at total destruction.

Thomas Maguire, owner of the Jenny Lind Theatre, was representative of many other building and business owners who lost property several times over during the course of these fires. His theatre was destroyed in all six! But Mr. Maguire was equally representative of the never-give-up attitude, and the common commitment, to carry on at all costs and against all odds. Every time, he shrugged his shoulders and rebuilt, restocked, and made new plans.

It isn't by chance that the fabled phoenix, rising from its own ashes, became a prominent feature of the city's official seal.

# CHAPTER 12

It was the fifth fire that destroyed the small adobe building that served as the headquarters of Joshua Norton & Company. Like so many other brave souls, Joshua and Peter were elsewhere, doing their best to help stop the advancing inferno. As good fortune would have it, much of their stored merchandise was safe in the hull of the old *Genessee* which remained outside of the fire's reach.

Joshua and Peter set about looking for a new location. Pickings were slim, and in great demand, as little was left standing.

Their immediate action paid off as they found an available space in an old granite building located at 110 Battery Street, which also housed the offices of several influential people, including the British Consul.

On his three lots at the intersection of Jackson and Sansome Streets, Joshua put in a rice mill, a cigar factory, and a frame building in which he rented small spaces to other businessmen.

It seemed, though, that if the fires didn't burn things down, then a series of earthquakes threatened to shake them up. One earthquake preceded the fifth great fire by only three days, and another broke windows and shook buildings only two weeks later. That one was so strong that even the ships anchored in the bay could feel its effects. Later that year, there were more strong jolts. In late 1852, the area was shaken so badly that the waters of Lake Merced sank over 30 feet as a chasm was produced which led from the lake to the ocean. In 1853 there were recorded more than thirty earthquakes of varying strength.

In the meantime, during this period of the early 1850's, there were great learning curves to be navigated. In the areas of health and safety, dealing with crime and criminals, in business, and in society and culture, the people of the city were moving forward. Homes and buildings were continually improved. Some improvements had to be modified as lessons were learned. The same was true for streets, sewers, and other public improvements. Despite the fires, areas of the city were graded and streets were planked. Although well behind the eight ball, more wharves were being constructed to manage the increase in maritime commerce.

Smack dab in the middle of all these fires, there was cause for a great deal of celebration. On September 9, 1850, California attained its statehood. The news didn't reach San Francisco until October 18, when the steamer *Oregon* sailed into the bay with guns a-blazing. The people were jubilant. October 29 was set aside as a day of celebration. Businesses closed, courts adjourned, and life-as-usual stopped for a short, happy time. Flags from every country under the sun were hoisted on the countless masts of ships in the bay and on the wharves. Bands played music and people danced in the streets. Bonfires were lighted up on the hills outside the city. A long-awaited dream had finally come true. They were now citizens of the United States.

# CHAPTER 13

It is now that I introduce to you the man to whom James Lick referred when Joshua and Peter came to rent his building. Sam Brannan will play an important part in the life of Joshua Norton.

Samuel Brannan, San Francisco's first huckster, and first millionaire, was born in Saco, Maine, in 1819. His family moved to Ohio when Sam was 14, and there he learned the printer's trade – which formed the basis of his professional life, but certainly not his fortune. He joined the Church of Jesus Christ of Latter Day Saints and moved to New York in 1844, where he started a church newspaper called *The Prophet*.

In February of 1846, he sailed, along with 240 other Mormons from New York, aboard the *Brooklyn*, bound for California by way of Cape Horn. He brought along an old printing press and a complete flour mill. Sailing via Honolulu in the Sandwich Islands, they ultimately landed in Yerba Buena on July 31, 1846.

He and his group tripled the population of the yet-small village.

Brannan established the first school in San Francisco (by then the name had been changed) and in 1847 he opened a supply store at Sutter's Fort – the location of the gold discovery.

In June, 1847, he traveled to Wyoming to meet with Brigham Young, head of the LDS Church, who was making his way west with a large group of Mormons. Brannan tried to encourage Young to bring his pioneers to San Francisco. Brigham Young rejected the idea, choosing, instead, to settle in Utah. Sam Brannan returned to Sutter's Fort.

Early in 1848, at the beginning of the Gold Rush, Brannan sold goods from his store to the miners and, as a representative of the LDS Church, he went to the mill to receive tithes from those members who were mining there. Word of this got to Brigham Young who wanted tithe money sent to him. Of course, Sam Brannan rejected that idea saying, "I'll send the money when the Lord sends a bill!" It was not forthcoming.

Brannan then went back to San Francisco, purchasing every shovel in the city and ran through the streets, holding up a bottle of gold dust, yelling, "Gold! Gold! Gold from the American River!"

His advertising methods were so successful that he opened more stores. In 1849, his store at Sutter's Fort, alone, sold $150,000 worth of supplies per month.

He was elected to the first town council of the City of San Francisco and shortly thereafter he went very public in his efforts to combat crime.

A barrel was placed at the corner of Clay and Montgomery Streets. Sam Brannan mounted it, and loudly denounced the marauding groups in the city, most notably the Sydney Ducks and another group made up of ex-New York volunteers, known as the "Hounds", whose primary activity was the persecution of foreigners in the city.

Sam Brannan worked up the crowds who sought revenge and he demanded that the lawlessness stop. If there was no law adequate enough to combat these criminals, he said, then these decent citizens would take the law into their own hands.

The challenges to the young City of San Francisco went far beyond the occurrences of earthquakes and fire. In fact, the fires, it is believed, were the result of very serious social ills to which the city was prone. There was disease – especially cholera – and there were the depraved practices of high-stakes gambling and women of ill repute which threatened the moral fabric of the city. There was much crime, including robberies and murders, plus the organized activities of groups of people such as the Hounds and the Ducks. This is where Sam Brannan's power came into its own. This all led to the formation of the Committee of Vigilance, and its inauguration with a hanging in Portsmouth Square one late night in June of 1851.

# CHAPTER 14

"You cannot hang him from there!"

Joshua Norton shouted as loud as he could to be heard above the din of the anxious crowd of onlookers. It was bad enough hanging this man in the first place, but he considered it scandalous to hang a man from the flagpole located in the center of Portsmouth Square.

"You cannot do that! What kind of message does that send? That flagpole has, from the very beginning, flown the flag of this country. If you hang him from there, from now until doomsday, every time we see the American flag flying above the square, all we will be able to think about is, 'That is where we hung John Jenkins back in '51'!"

About six hours earlier, John Jenkins had stolen a small safe out of the office of a shipping agent located at the Long Wharf on San Francisco Bay. A short time later, while making his getaway in a small boat, he was pursued, caught, beaten, shackled, and sent to a hastily-assembled court in the rooms of the newly-formed Committee of Vigilance on Battery Street, near the corner of Pine Street. The committee immediately found him guilty, but the members were reluctant to carry out the sentence (a conviction of grand larceny carried a penalty of death). They argued and wrangled about it until one of the members, Mr. William Howard, jumped up and said, "Gentlemen! As I understand it, we came here to hang somebody!" Mr. Howard's statement hit the right buttons, and suddenly they agreed. John Jenkins was dragged out of the building and down the street, passing hundreds of angry people. Entering Portsmouth Square, he was immediately taken over to the flagpole. One of the men holding the rope climbed the flagpole and strung the rope through the tackle block at the top.

It was then that Joshua intervened.

"Surely, you can find a more suitable place to carry out this execution!" he repeated.

After some animated discussion, they pulled down the rope, looked around the square, and dragged Jenkins over to the edge of the plaza, to the front of the old adobe custom house. There, an exposed beam provided ample support and height for the rope to be thrown over. Without hesitation, the men pulled on the rope, raising the thrashing body of John Jenkins and holding him there until the thrashing stopped and his body hung limp. The large crowd had gone completely quiet until now, and the silence was replaced by various jeers, cheers, tears, gasps of shock, and loud cries of grief. John Jenkins was dead. Justice had been served.

John Jenkins was one of the many ex-convicts from Australia who, having been released from prison in their home country, had come to San Francisco by the scores. They came to be known as the "Sydney Ducks", and were well known as troublemakers and hellraisers. Put simply, they were thugs, thieves and murderers.

Their actions over the previous year or so made them the prime suspects, as arsonists, for the fires that had plagued the city. And when caught for any crime, justice was easy to serve. John Jenkins' timing had not been good. He chose to commit his crime at the very time that the new Committee of Vigilance was being formed in order to fight crime in under-protected San Francisco.

Between July of 1849 and the time Joshua Norton arrived in San Francisco, in November, the population had swelled from a mere 5,000 to over 25,000. Yet, there remained only 34 law enforcement officers attempting to retain some semblance of order. By mid-1850, murders had doubled and robberies spiked dramatically. Confidence in the police force plummeted and the citizenry took it more and more upon themselves to administer justice.

By June of 1851, the discontent had increased to the point where prominent citizens decided to formally come together as a Committee of Vigilance. As they stated:

"We are determined that no thief, burglar, incendiary or assassin shall escape punishment either by the quibbles of the law, the insecurity of prison, the carelessness or corruption of police, or a laxity of those who pretend to administer justice."

The Committee of Vigilance was officially formed on June 9, 1851. When John Jenkins was executed, the ink on their charter had not even dried. Joshua Norton had not even had the chance yet to sign the roster, although he would, despite his reluctance to do so. As an upstanding member of the business community, he had no choice.

# CHAPTER 15

"So, you are going back to your Ithaca," said Joshua.

"No, to Baltimore," replied Peter, not understanding Joshua's reference. "Ithaca is a village in New York."

"I am speaking metaphorically. I mean YOUR Ithaca – as in Homer."

"Homer?" Peter was a little confused. He quickly tried to figure out who Joshua was talking about.

Joshua sensed his confusion. "You know. After fighting the Trojan War, Odysseus returns to his home of Ithaca; to his wife, Penelope; and to reclaim his title as King."

"Oh, HOMER!" said Peter.

"Bravo! You got it," said Joshua. "It took Odysseus, what – twenty years?"

"Yes, and he took the long way. Along his lengthy route he had to deal with Cyclops, Laestragonians, and sirens, among others. I hope it's easier to get back to Baltimore," said Peter.

"I have no doubt. That is, as long as your ship does not go the wrong way and get stranded on the rocks," said Joshua, with a chuckle. "But, what I mean is this: You have been traveling your own odyssey, sailing all the way to San Francisco, dealing with demons, such tragedies as fires, earthquakes, and the human demons of violence and unscrupulous individuals – plenty of those. You have had a great deal of success and made friends. I understand, though, that, like Odysseus, you have your 'Penelope' to go back to. In this case, to your family and your comfort, your familiarity and your safety. Not unlike many others whom this city and the gold fields have abused."

Joshua was right. One of the most prevalent diseases in Gold Rush San Francisco was homesickness. It led to deaths by the thousands.

Peter had been thinking about his decision for some time. His thoughts finally crystallized and his decision was made, and now he was in the midst of the most difficult part of the process – telling Joshua that he was leaving.

"I understand," said Joshua, "and I know you well enough to know that you are doing the right thing. I have nowhere to go and no one to go back to, so I am going to stay here and one day rule over this crazy empire. Just you wait and see, because if I were Emperor of the United States, you would see great changes effected, and everything would go harmoniously."

Joshua returned to the subject at hand. "You will be happy back home. I have no doubt of that. You will find a lady to marry and with whom to raise a family. You will have your church – your beloved St. Alphonsus – and your friends and, as you have proven here, you will be successful in business. In fact, I envy you, as you know who you are and where you came from. You have a family who loves you and you belong with them."

"I can handle hard work and difficulties in business and difficult people," said Peter. "but when the city burns down six times within the space of 18 months, I start to have doubts. On top of that, what doesn't burn down gets shaken to the ground in what you would call these "bloody" earthquakes. Then add in the mud, the rats, the garbage."

"And do not forget the fleas!" added Joshua.

"Oh, yes, the fleas! But the worst of it all is the senseless violence. I could never dream of such a thing, even in my worst nightmare. The beatings. The rapes. The murders. The horrible violence, in spite of the fact that they are foreigners from South America and China and wherever else! Then, having to watch people being hanged for their crimes, which seems equally barbaric."

Peter continued, "I know it's going to get better, and it is getting better, but I yearn for my family and the established city of Baltimore. Then, there's the subject of women, which we have talked about before. I'm sure you've noticed that there is a severe shortage of women around here – especially young women even approaching my age, and ones who aren't as strong and ugly as their husbands!"

Joshua laughed and nodded knowingly.

"Not to mention women who have some sense of morals and propriety, who actually behave like women. I have come to believe that there isn't one single woman in San Francisco that I would want to take back to Baltimore and introduce to my parents. Certainly, you know the challenges I have faced in that area of my life during these last two years."

"I do," said Joshua.

"But I thank you, Joshua. Your friendship has meant the world to me and the opportunities you have given to me and that we have created together.

I have created something of value and now good old Bill Sim, with your blessing, wants to buy my share, allowing me to go home to my family.

Joshua just stared out into space, his eyes beginning to betray a hint of moisture. He seemed in a trance – a bittersweet trance – but then he broke the silence:

> *Breathes there a man with soul so dead*
> *Who never to himself hath said,*
> *This is my own, my native land!*
> *Whose heart hath ne'er within him burned,*
> *As home his footsteps he hath turned*
> *From wandering on a foreign strand!*
> *If there such breathe, go, mark him well ...*

Peter made arrangements to leave San Francisco. After a great deal of research and speaking with the right people, he was able to book passage on one of the few ships leaving San Francisco, returning to New York. A few weeks passed before his day of departure became reality.

"I have a going away present for you," said Joshua.

"And I have a gift for you," said Peter.

Joshua spoke: "Through all these weeks and months we have worked together, I have known it was difficult for you as a virile young man in this seemingly God-forsaken city. You are certainly of marrying age, and as you are so young and good-looking, it would be a waste for you not to find a good wife and raise a family. It is no secret that I am fond of the writings of William Shakespeare, and I had brought with me this small leather-bound copy of his sonnets. I want you to have it. As you may or may not know, the first sixteen sonnets are written to a handsome young man, much like you. In them, Shakespeare is telling him that it would be a sin for such a fellow to not reproduce himself. His abstinence would rob the world of his beauty for the ages."

Joshua opened the book and read from Sonnet Number Three:

> *Look in thy glass, and tell the face thou viewest*
> *Now is the time that face should form another:*
> *Whose fresh repair if now thou not renewest,*
> *Thou dost beguile the world, unbless some mother.*

*For where is she so fair whose unear'd womb*
*Disdains the tillage of thy husbandry?*
*Or who is he so fond will be the tomb*
*Of his self-love, to stop posterity?*
*Thou art thy mother's glass, and she in thee*
*Calls back the lovely April of her prime:*
*So thou through windows of thine age shall see,*
*Despite of wrinkles this thy golden time.*
*But if thou live, remember'd not to be,*
*Die single, and thine image dies with thee.*

"So heed his words. Go home. Find the right woman to share you with the world!"

Then it was Peter's turn to give Joshua a gift.

"This seemingly pales in comparison to your gift, but I believe it has great significance."

With that, Peter reached into his pocket and pulled out a small coin which he placed in Joshua's hand. Joshua held it up to his eyes and gazed upon an 1828 French franc, bearing the likeness of King Charles X. Joshua had told him about his beliefs regarding his childhood and his "true" family history.

Joshua took in a quick breath of air, as in surprise. Before he could say a word, Peter jumped in.

"The other day I was at the El Dorado Gambling Hall. There, amidst all the tables piled high with gold, was one table where a gentleman was displaying his collection of foreign coins. They had been culled from among all the coins that had crossed the tables in the form of bets in games of faro or monte. As I was looking them over, my eyes gazed upon this French franc, and I was transfixed by the profile displayed on the coin. I thought how much that looks like you! Especially the shape of your nose, if you don't mind me saying that. The man saw me staring at the coin. He said that was King Charles X, the last of the Bourbon Kings. Then my curiosity really piqued. I remembered you spoke to me of being of the Bourbon royalty. So I had to have it. I offered to buy it, and he agreed, especially since his price was far more than the face value of the coin. I felt the coin was worth more than that in the meaning it would have for you!"

Joshua was nearly speechless. The gift of this simple coin meant more than he could ever say. It meant that Peter had really listened to him during those few times that Joshua had bared his soul to him. As a symbol of their friendship, it was more valuable than all the piles of gold at the El Dorado.

Joshua fell silent for a time. Tears welled up in his eyes, and he literally began to shake, as though shivering from the cold. He turned the coin over and over, examining it carefully, rubbing his fingers over the high-relief image of the king. It was a long time before he spoke, but when he finally overcame his emotions he looked Peter directly in the eyes and simply said, "You understand. You understand. You are the only one who understands."

It was a very touching moment. Peter's gesture had hit the mark. What a bittersweet moment as their time together was coming to an end.

Joshua looked at Peter, his eyes moist with emotion, and said:

> *"Where'er I roam, whatever realms to see,*
> *My heart untraveled, fondly turns to thee,*
> *Still to my brother turns, with ceaseless pain,*
> *And drags at each remove a lengthening chain."*

"That's very profound," said Peter.

"Yes, but that is not me. That is Oliver Goldsmith. This is me:

"You have been like a son – I have taught you and helped you be successful in business. I feel like I have contributed in a positive way as you have matured into such a fine young man.

"You have been like a brother – we have shared so many experiences. And you have taught me, as well, and have influenced me with your youthful enthusiasm.

"But, most of all, you have been a friend – a good, good friend.

"And thank you for this coin – this wonderful, meaningful memento of our friendship. I shall cherish it until my dying day."

# CHAPTER 16

Eventually, Joshua bought four parcels of land in North Beach slated to be developed by a man named Henry Meiggs. In fact he was so optimistic about the prospects, he purchased four more, in partnership with another gentleman.

Henry Meiggs had a good reputation. He saw to that! He was quite the glad-hander, but what Joshua and others didn't know at the time was that if you shake hands with him, you'd better hold your other hand over your wallet. Joshua didn't have a lot to with Henry Meiggs, at least not directly, but Meiggs had a rather strong impact upon the course of Joshua's life.

Henry Meiggs was born in New York in 1811. By the time he was in his mid-twenties, he was a wealthy man, having purchased a lumber mill in Brooklyn.

In the 1840's things got a little difficult for him back east, and he decided to come out west. He purchased a sailing vessel, loaded it with lumber, and sailed around the Horn, arriving in San Francisco in July of 1849.

Meiggs sold his lumber quickly, and for a very large sum of money. With his profits he built, among other things, a sawmill and a large wharf in North Beach. In the meantime he used his ship to make regular trips back and forth bringing lumber from the East Coast.

In 1850, a clipper ship, the *Frolic*, sank among the rocks off the California Coast near Point Cabrillo, just north of San Francisco. The *Frolic*, a former opium-runner, had been on the way from China to San Francisco, this time loaded with Chinese lacquered tables, marble, porcelain, silver tinderboxes, and gold filigree jewelry, among many other treasures. Henry Meiggs, learning of the shipwreck, sent an expedition of ships up the coast hoping to salvage some of this treasure. While he didn't find anything from the *Frolic*, he did discover a large stand of gigantic redwood trees growing along the river. Never the one to let opportunity pass him by, Meiggs had a steam-powered lumber mill shipped from the East Coast and placed it in the town he founded, which he named Meiggsville (today it is known as Mendocino).

Meiggs was a very successful businessman. Handsome. Well-liked. Trusted. Generous. In fact, people gladly gave him the nickname "Honest Harry". He was elected a city alderman, and he became a solid member of the community. Later, in 1854, along with concert-pianist Rudolph Herold, he formed the San Francisco Philharmonic Society.

Honest Harry Meiggs bought up a great deal of land in North Beach. Naturally, wanting to improve it quickly, he lobbied to have the city build a tunnel under Stockton Street, to create an easy way for people to get to North Beach. They rejected the idea. So Honest Harry Meiggs used his own money to grade Stockton and Powell streets, extending them through the sand dunes which separated North Beach from the city.

If that wasn't enough, he then built a road starting at Montgomery Street extending around the base of Telegraph Hill and ending in – you guessed it – North Beach. At that point, Honest Harry built his famous pier – known as Meiggs' Wharf – which extended 2,000 feet into the bay. In order to attract more people to the area, he convinced his friend, Abe Warner, to build an amusement house on the wharf. He did so, and called it the Cobweb Palace.

In order to pay for all of his improvements, Honest Harry subdivided his North Beach land and put the lots up for sale. Unfortunately by this time – 1854 – San Francisco had entered an era of economic depression. Very few lots sold.

How was Honest Harry Meiggs going to pay for all his improvements, his high-interest loans, his property taxes, and his assessments?

Honest Harry got hold of a large supply of blank city promissory notes – many of which were already signed by the mayor. With these notes, he began to pay his debts. When the pre-signed notes ran out, he started forging signatures on the others.

Honest Harry Meiggs worried about getting caught, so he decided to take pre-emptive action. He bought a small brig and, on October 6, 1854, loaded it with provisions, ostensibly to take his family out for a day's sail on the bay. However, he and his family sailed out through the Golden Gate, heading west, and into the horizon, taking with him an additional $800,000 in cash that he had embezzled, and leaving behind about $1,000,000 in personal debts. His timing was incredible. Had he been willing and able to look back, he would have seen the city fathers of San Francisco discovering, that very day, his indiscretions.

Needless to say, Joshua was thunderstruck by the criminal nerve of that boastful, boor of a man.

"Henry Meiggs can go to the dogs!" he said. "If I were Emperor, I would have him thrown into the dungeon!"

# CHAPTER 17

China was the main supplier of rice to California until a famine cut off shipments. As a result of the scarcity, the price was driven from only four cents per pound up to 36 cents per pound – a 900% increase. Owing especially to the number of Chinese workers in the area, there was great demand.

Joshua, like many other speculators, conducted his business at the Merchant's Exchange. Located there was a mercantile bank known as Goddefroy & Sillem which acted as agent for the Ruiz brothers, from South America. The Ruiz brothers owned a ship called the *Glyde,* which was sitting in San Francisco Bay loaded to its scuppers with 200,000 pounds of rice from Peru.

"Have I got a deal for you!" said Willy Sillem to Joshua. "You can have the entire shipload of rice for only twelve and a half cents per pound. It's sitting right there in the bay just waiting for someone with the foresight to seize upon this deal. At $25,000 for the shipload, you could sell it for 36 cents a pound and gross $72,000! That's almost a 300% profit!"

Peter, unfortunately, was no longer at his side to help Joshua ask the right questions. Peter would have asked the obvious: "If it's such a good deal, why don't you just sell it to someone for 36 cents per pound?"

Joshua was not so careful. In a very weak moment, he said yes to the deal and, on December 22, 1852, paid a $2,000 cash down payment, signing a contract promising to pay the balance in thirty days.

The very next day, a ship called the *Syren* sailed into San Francisco Bay, loaded with rice from Peru. The news hit Joshua like a shot. Then, over the next few days, several more ships arrived, each one with its holds filled to the top with rice. The *Merceditas*. The *Dragon*. On and on, like a Gatling gun, each ship a painful shot to the gut. In less than a week, there was an unbelievable glut of rice in San Francisco.

The price plummeted to 3 cents per pound. Joshua was devastated. He attempted to nullify the contract based on the fact that Willy Sillem had lied to him.

"Bait and switch, that is what it was," he said. "Sillem's sample of rice that he showed me, and upon which the sale was based, was of a much higher grade than what I found on the *Glyde*."

The Ruiz brothers sued Joshua for the $23,000 due them under the contract. The court battle lasted over two years and, of course, the legal bills mounted.

Bill Sim, the Scotsman who had taken over Peter's interest in Joshua Norton & Company, was no moral support at all. In fact, he was no support of any kind, as he tucked his tail between his legs and got out of town as fast as a boat could take him. He was never heard from again.

Joshua was left alone to fight his battle.

In 1855, the court finally ruled against Joshua. By then, the Gold Rush was over. The flow of gold from the fields was now a trickle. Prices of just about everything crashed. The real estate market collapsed. Businesses closed. Banks failed. Bankruptcy was common, and Joshua Norton, along with scores of other hapless souls, was ruined.

The bank foreclosed on his North Beach properties. He had to sell his business and his properties at Sansome and Jackson Streets at a huge loss, and what he did receive immediately went toward his legal expenses.

To add insult to injury, Joshua was falsely accused of embezzlement by a former client. He had to use his Rincon Point properties as collateral for a loan to fight the charge.

He moved from his current lodgings to a simpler boarding house on Montgomery Street, run by a Mrs. Rutledge.

Joshua Norton, never a quitter, was eventually able to move beyond his legal problems – those having finally been put to rest. With help from a few sympathetic businessmen, he was allowed to sell a few commodities on a commission basis. He earned enough to be able to meet his daily needs and, in fact, upgraded his lodgings, moving to the Tehama House (formerly the Jones Hotel where he once lived) which new owners had modestly upgraded from its previous condition.

# CHAPTER 18

Not only was Joshua Norton in dire straits, so was the City of San Francisco. The glory days of the Gold Rush were, indeed, over and the world came crashing down. Businesses, banks, and real estate spiraled into the abyss. Supply far exceeded demand, and unclaimed shipments languished and rotted on the wharves. Joshua Norton was only one of many who were suffering.

Occasionally, a newspaper advertisement would show up identifying Joshua as a commission agent, offering his services as broker for sales of coffee, barley and other goods. But that didn't last long, and eventually it seemed as though this once-successful businessman disappeared from the face of the earth. He had lost his spirit.

What was he left with?

Over everything was his abiding belief that he was born of royalty and had been cheated out of his due.

He had no family. Even his friend and partner, Peter Robertson, had gone home to Baltimore. Joshua was completely alone.

He had seen the dishonest prosper, and the honest trampled. For him, reality seemed to be turned upside down.

Then, during his long wilderness years, the city began to change before his eyes.

The old, small city Joshua knew was transforming itself into a full-fledged metropolitan city. Cleansed by fire and earthquake, the tents and shanties had virtually disappeared, replaced with large solid buildings of brick and granite. San Francisco was beginning to look more like the mature cities of the east.

The city also developed a spirit of permanence. Those who had prospered during the Gold Rush, and survived the downturn of the mid-50's, were now wanting to set down roots, to build, and to grow their future in the City of San Francisco.

But Joshua Norton had been crushed. The damage had been done. He was feeling more and more like a fish out of water. Ironically, he had prospered during the wild, chaotic, challenging times of the Gold Rush years, and now as San Francisco was maturing into a first-class city, his grasp of reality was slipping. His delusion came more and more to the forefront of his consciousness.

In the larger scheme of things, the winds carried doubt and uncertainty on the state and federal level as well. The Civil War was looming on the horizon.

Back in Washington D.C., some feared that California would break away from the Union and join with the southern states. Others feared that California might, along with Oregon and Washington, form its own sovereign nation – totally independent from the United States.

Locally, in California, there was a move to divide the state into two separate states, severing it at the 36th parallel. Andres Pico, formerly a Spanish citizen, born at San Diego in what was then known as New Spain, was now a citizen of the United States and a member of the California State Assembly. In February, 1859, he authored what was known as the Pico Act, designed to divide the state and turn the southern half into what would be known as "The Territory of Colorado", which would become a slave-holding state. The Pico Act was passed by both houses of the California Legislature, and signed by the governor. But, fortunately, was never acted upon by the U. S. Congress.

As the decade of the '50's came to an end, California was affected even more personally by the debate over slavery. State Supreme Court Justice David S. Terry gave a vitriolic speech denouncing U.S. Senator David C. Broderick and arguing against those who supported the abolition of slavery. Broderick retaliated, referring to Terry as "that damned miserable wretch."

A duel was challenged, and Terry shot Broderick, killing him.

That was on September 13, 1859. For Joshua Norton it was the last straw. It was the final act that sent his mind over the edge and compelled him to realize what he was convinced was his true calling in life.

He remembered Old Moses, in his tattered army uniform, walking the streets of Cape Town and decrying the state of the world. He had the right idea, thought Joshua, but he only talked about it.

"I am going to actually do something about it!" he exclaimed.

# CHAPTER 19

It had been said, "That's what happens when you prevent someone from doing what they do best. They go insane."

Joshua Norton did not go insane, but he filled an emptiness in his life with his delusion of royalty. He could no longer be a titan of business. He could no longer successfully buy and sell commodities. He could no longer deal with the cruelties and injustices of the world. He could only survive if, even only in his own mind, he was in charge. He had to make the rules, even if no one listened to him or heeded his words.

Joshua's wilderness years were over because he had made up his mind that it was time he fulfilled his purpose in life. He was of royal blood, he had no doubt about that, and by putting himself forth as the emperor, he was doing a great favor for the people of San Francisco. They would be his subjects and he would be their beneficent ruler. As his first act, he would issue an official proclamation to that effect.

After several days of thinking about his proclamation, he spent all night writing and revising it so that it correctly expressed his intentions, and those he thought to be the will of the people. So, on the morning of September 17, 1859, Joshua Norton put on his blue uniform jacket, with the brass buttons, his red trimmed military cap, and walked to 517 Clay Street, the office of the *California Bulletin* newspaper. Asking to speak with the editor, he was ushered, by the receptionist, into the office of Mr. George Kenyon Fitch, who stood up from behind his desk, leaned over, and extended his hand.

Joshua hesitantly shook his hand, fidgeted a bit, and fumbled with the paper clenched in his left hand. Realizing his posture was making him look weak, he suddenly jerked to attention, his stocky frame suddenly appearing strong and assured. He thrust the paper toward Mr. Fitch who accepted it politely.

"I would be most appreciative," Joshua said with great confidence, "if you would read this document and further, I respectfully request that you publish it in this evening's edition of your very fine newspaper."

"Well, I'll be happy to read it," said Mr. Fitch. "Whether or not I can print it will depend on a number of things, and ..."

"I understand," said Joshua, interrupting his statement. "I will leave you now to peruse it. I thank you very much for your time. You have been very kind to receive me."

With that, Joshua politely bowed his head and walked out the door, stopping to thank the receptionist for her graciousness.

"Who is the lovely lady to whom I am so indebted for her kindness?" he asked.

She looked around and then caught herself, realizing he was speaking about her.

"Oh, my goodness, thank you!" she said. "I'm Gladys Watson, Mr. Fitch's receptionist."

"He is a very fortunate man," said Joshua Norton as he exited.

"What a strange little man," she said after he had gone out. "But what a nice gentleman he was."

Glancing at the paper, Mr. Fitch said, "Apparently he is not just a gentleman, Miss Watson. According to this, he is the Emperor of the United States!"

Mr. Fitch carefully read the document that had been handed to him. He read it again. Then again, a third time. He chuckled, and he laughed.

"What is this fellow up to?" he asked himself. "While he seemed slightly hesitant at first, and his eyes looked slightly glazed, he certainly had a serious demeanor and a regal bearing. Somehow, I strangely liked him."

As it happened, it was a slow news day, and Mr. Fitch, taking this all as a joke decided to be a part of the joke, and not a victim. So in that day's edition he ran the following headline:

### *Have We an Emperor Among Us?*

On the front page in a prominent position, he printed the proclamation he had been given:

> At the peremptory request of a large majority of the citizens of these United States, I, Joshua Norton, formerly of Algoa Bay, Cape of Good Hope, and now for the past nine years and ten months of San Francisco, California, declare and proclaim myself Emperor of these U.S., and in virtue of the authority thereby in me vested, **DO HEREBY** order and direct the representatives of the different States of the Union to assemble in the Musical Hall of this city on the 1st day of February next, then and there to make such alterations in the existing laws of the Union as may ameliorate the evils under which the country is laboring, and thereby cause confidence to

*exist, both at home and abroad, in our stability and*
*integrity.*

*Signed: NORTON I*
*Emperor of the United States*

The horse was out of the barn and there was no turning back.

Joshua Norton no longer existed. From this point on he was Emperor Norton, or Norton I. If you were to call him Joshua or Mr. Norton, you would be politely corrected.

The Emperor was greatly pleased – and a little surprised – when he saw the evening edition of the *California Bulletin*. There was his proclamation – and on the front page, thank you very much! To the question, "Have We an Emperor Among Us?" the answer was a resounding "Yes!" The emperor was ready to meet his subjects and to watch over the people of his empire.

For his first official proclamation as Emperor, Norton decided to abolish the Congress of the United States. He had been increasingly upset by the ineptitude and unfairness of this body of men.

Since Mr. Fitch had been so kind to him, and since, of course, his royal patronage had already greatly increased the circulation of his humble newspaper, the Emperor returned to the offices of the *Bulletin* giving them the opportunity to publish this important proclamation.

"Good morning, Miss Watson," said the Emperor, as he bowed and proffered her the single white rose he held in his hand.

Blushing, Gladys Watson accepted his gift with grace and dignity, much to the Emperor's liking.

"Oh, thank you sir – Your Majesty!" she said. "What a nice uniform you are wearing today."

Emperor Norton was wearing his same uniform – the navy blue military jacket covered with brass buttons, but now he had placed large tarnished golden epaulets on the shoulders. His dark brown leather boots were greatly in need of polishing. He carried his soft, red-trimmed cap in his hands, having respectfully removed it upon entering the office.

"You are very kind, Miss Watson. If you would kindly see that Mr. Fitch receives this newest proclamation in a timely manner, I would be equally obliged."

"Yes, sir," she said. "He is not in at the moment, but I will place it in a prominent position on his desk and upon his return I will make sure he is aware of its existence."

"Thank you for your service, Miss Watson. Now, if you will excuse me, I will leave you to your business."

With that, Emperor Norton turned and disappeared onto the street.

Again, like a well-oiled royal gazette, the *Bulletin* published the Emperor's newest proclamation. The headline read:

### Congress Abolished! Take Notice, the World!

*His Imperial Majesty, Norton I, has issued the following edict, which he desires the Bulletin to spread before the world. Let her rip!*

*It is reported to us that the universal suffrage, as now existing throughout the Union, is abused; that fraud and corruption prevent a fair and proper expression of the public voice; that open violation of the laws are constantly occurring, caused by mobs, parties, factions and undue political sects; that the citizen has not that protection of person and property which he is entitled to by paying his pro rata of the expense of the Government – in consequence of which, WE do hereby abolish Congress, and it is therefore abolished; and WE order and desire the representatives of all parties interested to appear at the Music Hall of*

*this city on the first of February next, and then and
there take the most effective steps to remedy the evil
complained of.*

*Signed: NORTON I
Emperor of the United States*

Needless to say, no one showed up.

In succeeding days and weeks, Emperor Norton produced a
staggering series of proclamations – all hand-written on borrowed
letterhead from various hotels, clubs, and associations. They
included the following:

- He discharged the Governor of Virginia (whom he
  determined to be insane) for hanging John Brown.

- Since Congress had not disbanded in accordance with his
  previous decree, Norton ordered the Commander of the
  Armies of the U.S. to clear the halls of congress.

- Unhappy with the whole lot of the country's governing
  officials, Norton dissolved the Republic of the United States
  in favor of an Absolute Monarchy.

On this last point, he had planned a speech (never actually
given) which was printed in the *Bulletin* newspaper. In it he said:
"Taking all circumstances into consideration, and the internal
dissensions on slavery, we are certain that nothing will save the
nation from utter ruin except an absolute monarchy under the
supervision and authority of an independent Emperor."

You can guess who the absolute monarch was to be.

# CHAPTER 20

By 1863, Emperor Norton had moved into his permanent home (it was to be so for the rest of his life) in the Eureka Lodgings located at 624 Commercial Street, between Montgomery and Kearny. He paid 50 cents per day for a 9' by 6' room, third floor front. It had a view of the narrow street by means of the small window at the far end of the room. This afforded a modicum of fresh air, yet also allowed a constant din from all the activity which took place there.

His furniture consisted of a small iron cot with rickety springs, an old saggy armchair, a soiled couch, a wash basin, and a night table. Needless to say, there was room for little else, including a closet, so his clothes were hung on "ten penny" nails pounded into the walls. A threadbare carpet, barely visible, covered the floor. A few lithographs, notably of royalty, filled the blank spaces on the walls. The faces which stared at him every morning included those of Queen Victoria, Empress Carlotta of Mexico, Queen Emma of the Sandwich Islands, and Empress Eugenie, the wife of Napoleon III.

The Emperor was emaciated, having not eaten well for some time. He benefited from the gifts of money from kind former business associates – those he had not alienated during the difficult times – and from his fellow Freemasons, among whom he had been a fellow member ever since his salad days of the early '50's. Norton didn't like taking charity, so in order to save face, he treated these gifts as either taxes collected from his citizens or as "tributes" given to him by his loving, loyal subjects.

Emboldened by the payments of these taxes and tributes, Emperor Norton began visiting local businesses, soliciting occasional "tax" payments. Most refused to pay, and he was gracious in defeat as much as in victory. Over time, more and more businessmen good naturedly paid him. It was at this time that the practice of the royal warrant came into being. As his fame increased, restaurants and other businesses found that by associating themselves with Emperor Norton, they received a great deal of publicity and their respective businesses prospered. Small payments of cash (taxes), free meals, or whatever, were a small price to pay. Signs and placards began appearing which stated that these various businesses enjoyed the patronage of the Emperor. "Gentlemen's Outfitters to His Imperial Majesty", "By Appointment to His Majesty, the Emperor", and, even though he never took a sip of wine or alcohol, "Fine Wines and Spirits by Appointment to His Majesty, Norton The First".

On a typical day, Emperor Norton would rise early, as was his discipline, and would dress in his uniform. The condition of his clothes varied, as they mostly consisted of well-worn uniforms given to him by Army officers at the Presidio, or, occasionally, were old uniforms purchased from Pacific Street auction houses. He intended for his uniforms to be worn at formal and official occasions, but since he was on duty every day, there was virtually never a time that he was not seen in his official dress.

The Emperor would pull on a pair of old trousers and select a shirt – hopefully not too torn – which he would tuck into his waist. Then on would come his old brown boots. As of now, they fit rather well. In time, he would cut slits in the leather in order to accommodate the corns which developed on his feet. Over his shirt, he would put on his blue army officer's coat, adorned with epaulets of tarnished gold and covered, on the front, with gold buttons.

This seemed to suffice, but certain days required just a few more touches, from a simple flower in his buttonhole, if available, or, for really important occasions, he would strap a cavalry sword onto his hips.

Normally, he would have put on a kepi – a soft, flat topped cap which had been a staple in his dress, but recently he had been gifted with a tall, black beaver hat complete with rosette and an ostrich plume which quickly became the pride of his wardrobe.

One final touch, selected as he would exit his room, was his knotty wood walking stick with its ornate handle. On rainy days, or days which promised the possibility of such, he would also grab his lacquered Chinese umbrella.

Emperor Norton's days followed a regular pattern. After dressing, he would step downstairs to pay his fifty-cent rent. He would then go next door to the Empire Hotel where he enjoyed reading the morning newspaper. If the occasion permitted, he would converse with guests of the hotel about various subjects, from current events, to history, literature, or – among his favorite subjects – science and engineering.

He would then stroll down the street, inspecting sidewalks, roadways, buildings, signs, and what have you to determine their conditions and make sure there were no hazards. It was serious business keeping after the public works department and protecting the safety of his citizens. He visited markets, and docks, and any buildings in the area that were under construction.

The Emperor would work his way towards Portsmouth Square where he regularly visited with friends and listen for the noonday bell in the tower of St. Mary's Church. It would signal time for lunch – often at his favorite place, Martin & Horton's on Clay Street. He had the freedom of virtually every restaurant in the city, and although a non-drinker, of virtually every saloon, such as Barry and Patten, The Bank Exchange, Franks, or the Pantheon, where he was offered free lunches, even though he eschewed the normally-required purchase of a drink.

Emperor Norton's afternoons were usually spent back at Portsmouth Square, where the world of San Francisco congregated. He would sit on a park bench and visit with friends, especially his "Grand Chamberlain" (as the newspaper referred to him), his Chinese friend, Ah How. If it was cold or inclement, the Emperor would spend his afternoon in a library; at the Bohemian Club, the Mercantile Institute, or at the Mechanics' Institute. At any of these locations, he would wile away the afternoon reading books or magazines, playing chess (which he played very well), or writing his proclamations using their fancy, engraved stationery. This always helped give his words added weight.

The Emperor loved children and young people, and believed strongly in higher education. Once in a while he would be invited to visit a school, inspect its facilities, and speak with the students. He was often invited to school commencements, where he felt just as much pride in the graduates as did their parents.

Evenings would find him attending debating societies, lectures, or the theatre – where complimentary seating awaited his royal presence.

On Sundays, Emperor Norton went to church. On one Sunday he might attend Old St. Mary's. Another Sunday might find him at the Episcopalian Grace Cathedral. He would attend the First Unitarian Church to hear the sermons of his favorite preacher, Rev. Horatio Stebbins. On Saturdays, he would sometimes attend Temple Emmanu-El. Norton once told a minister, "I think it is my duty to encourage religion and morality by showing myself at church. In order to avoid jealousy, I attend them all, in turn!"

Emperor Norton's feelings about the universality of all religion were so strong that he eventually issued a proclamation to this effect:

> "**WHEREAS** *there are great commotions in different quarters of the terrestrial globe, arising from discussing the question, 'The Purification of the Bible – its Truths and False Lights', and fears are entertained that a war may break out at some remote point and spread all over the world, carrying in its winding course death, pestilence, famine, devastation and ruin;*
>
> **WHEREAS** *such a state of affairs is to be deplored by all liberal-minded Christians, who oppose bigotry, charlatanism, and humbuggery, and who follow the golden maxim of the lamented Lincoln, "With malice toward none – with charity for all";*
>
> **AND WHEREAS**, *Religion is like a beautiful garden, wherein the False Lights may be compared to the poppies, which fall to the ground, decay and are no more, the True Lights bloom in everlasting etherealism, blessing forever the Creator and the Christian world by their Love and Truth;*
>
> **NOW THEREFORE**, *we, Norton I (etc.), do hereby command all communities select delegates to a Bible Convention, to be held in the City of San Francisco, State of California, U.S.A… for the purpose of eliminating all doubtful passages contained in the present printed edition of the Bible, and that measures be adopted towards the obliteration of all religious sects and the establishment of an Universal Religion.*"

Emperor Norton, if nothing else, was a tireless advocate of everyone getting together and forgetting differences. Reason and tolerance were the keys to universal brotherhood.

In his middle age, Emperor Norton was a picturesque and striking figure – especially as his "fortunes" increased and he was able to dine in the manner to which he became accustomed. His moustache and beard were becoming of a royal personage. It was a striking and obvious reality that he bore a resemblance to Napoleon III.

Looking like a king, regally carrying himself like a king, and caring for his people as he did, in the form of a benevolent king, Emperor Norton truly enjoyed his position and his self-determined calling in life. He helped countless people solve their problems by listening to their complaints, and ruling on disputes like Solomon. He constantly looked out for everyone's best interest and shared his knowledge for their benefit. He was in no way overbearing nor a bore. He never permitted himself to be regarded as a nuisance. He knew when to appear and when to retire.

Let us not forget his economic value to the city. Emperor Norton was a draw for the tourists. Many came to see him, to meet him, to get his autograph, and to purchase those Emperor Norton Souvenirs hawked by many vendors: post cards, dolls, pennants, and prints of his likeness.

The Emperor never tired of this adulation, the respect, and, especially, the free meals!

# CHAPTER 21

Now, here's my favorite part. It's when I enter to play my part in this story!

One of San Francisco's annalists wrote that out of the mist came Sam Brannan, and up from the mud arose Emperor Norton. James Lick appeared, and then came ... Mark Twain! I don't know where he thinks I came from!

I had just recently adopted my pen name. My friends and acquaintances still knew me as Samuel Clemens – but I proudly answered to both.

Here's the story of my first days in San Francisco, and how I met the Emperor:

In June of 1864 I was asked by my friend, George Barnes, to come out to San Francisco and take a position of local reporter for the *Morning Call* newspaper. As it happened, the *Morning Call* building was right next door to the Eureka Lodgings, where

Emperor Norton lived in his very small third-floor room. The Eureka Lodgings were squeezed in between the *Morning Call* building and the Empire Hotel – all sharing frontage on the very noisy and narrow Commercial Street. Our newsroom was on the third floor of the building, right next door to the Emperor, and we shared our floor with the United States Branch Mint. Rather wealthy company! Running the mint were Superintendent Robert B. Swain, and his secretary, Francis Bret Harte, whom we have all come to know and love as the great writer, Bret Harte. Bret and I became very good friends – at the time. It was ironic, though, that the Mint was right next door to Emperor Norton's room, because back in '51, when he was a successful and wealthy businessman, he petitioned to have a mint be built in San Francisco. It finally arrived, and he lived right next door, but he was too poor to take advantage of it.

I moved to San Francisco with my friend, Steve Gillis. Me and Steve moved around a bit, but for a time we settled with a family on Minna Street, living in a room at the back of the house. I was happy to be in such a quiet place, until their flea-bitten hound started to howl. One morning, Steve found me standing in the doorway with a revolver pointed at the offending dog. It was so damn cold that I couldn't get a bead on him. Steve said, "Don't shoot him, Sam, just swear at him. You can easily kill him at that range with your profanity!" I did so. I let go a scorching blast of profanity (which I wouldn't repeat here), that so traumatized the brute that his owner promptly sold him and replaced him with a Mexican hairless dog!

Please forgive my digression. I know this isn't about me. But I tell that little story to show that there is a darker side of my soul, whereas when it came to the Emperor, I was always on my best behavior. While others made fun of him and ridiculed his sad status, I found a great deal to admire about him. I thought he was a lovable old humbug!

But, oh, dear, it was always a painful thing to me to see Emperor Norton begging, although he later found ways to "earn" a living by selling his promissory notes to well-meaning subjects (I'll tell you about that later). And he certainly earned his keep in his services to the betterment of this community. Although nobody else believed he was an Emperor, he believed it. Those who have written about him were only able to see his ludicrous or grotesque side. I was able to see more than this.

I believe that whenever you find yourself on the side of the majority, it is time to pause and reflect. So I must be right. I am in the minority on this subject, and I think there was a pathetic side to him. I have seen the Emperor when his dignity was wounded – in fact I have seen him in all his various moods and tenses, and there was always more room for pity than for laughter. I liked him, and respected him.

I met the Emperor for the first time out on the crowded, bustling street in front of our respective buildings. I was returning from a reporting assignment for the "lokulitems" as I liked to call them, and Emperor Norton was headed next door to the Empire Hotel to read the morning papers. It was not difficult to know this was the Emperor heading my way. He was easy to spot with his blue jacket covered with brass buttons and shoulders topped with its tarnished gold epaulets.

"Good morning, Emperor Norton," I said, bowing respectfully, as I understood was the proper thing to do.

"Good morning," said the Emperor. "You are Mr. Mark Twain, are you not?"

"Guilty!" was my simple reply.

Emperor Norton chuckled. "I recognize you from your likeness which accompanies your column in the newspaper. I must tell you, I greatly enjoy your writing and your valuable contribution to the community."

"Thank you, Your Majesty. You are very kind."

"It is heartfelt," said the Emperor.

"I have been complimented many times by many people," I said. "And they embarrass me; I always feel that they have not said enough!"

Emperor Norton laughed. "Would you like me to continue? I could be more effusive with my praise."

It was my turn to laugh. "No, thank you. Too much praise and I'll pop my buttons with pride – and I can't afford that 'cause I don't have near as many buttons on my coat as you do! Well, if you'll excuse me, Your Majesty, I have to file a story with the newspaper."

We parted ways. I had to post a story at The *Morning Call*, and the Emperor left to make his rounds, visit with friends, and make his contributions to the colorful life in San Francisco.

On many a day, our paths would cross – most often right there on Commercial Street where our separate worlds intersected – but occasionally in other areas of the city as we were independently meddling in the lives of other people.

On one occasion, in July, 1864, I think it was, I had been planning an excursion out to the Cliff House, located on the far reaches of the peninsula where the land meets the sea. I had been told that the only time such a trip could be enjoyed thoroughly was early in the morning. My friend Harry, the stock-broker was already on board, and I decided to ask the Emperor if he would be interested in going. Even after advising him that I was sure it wasn't going to be in a royal carriage, and that having never done this before, I could make no promises as to what would unfold, he immediately said "Yes!".

The following morning, Harry and the Emperor and I met at the stable at the ungodly hour of four o'clock.

I was going to write an article about this trip for the newspaper, and had several desires regarding our day's experience. Here's what I had planned: An early trip with smooth sailing on a road unencumbered by carriages, free from wind and dust; a bracing early-morning atmosphere; the spectacle of the sun rising behind us and lighting the way before us; the fresh perfume of flowers still damp with dew; a solitary drive on the ocean beach; and a vision of white sails glinting in the morning light far out at sea.

As I reported, here is what we experienced:

We all yawned and stretched, trying to wake up as the horse was hitched up to the buggy. Once it was ready, we hopped aboard and exited the stable, going out into the bracing atmosphere. In the article I remember saying that if another such voyage were proposed to me, I would want it understood that there was to be no bracing atmosphere in the program. Within a half hour, we were so thoroughly "braced", that we came within a scratch of being frozen to death.

The road was not encumbered by carriages, and for good reason. We paid our 75-cent toll to use the roadway, and wondered who else would be so foolhardy to be out there in such conditions. The wind was cold, coming straight in from the ocean, and it blew with such force that we could hardly make any headway. I was sure there were icebergs out there somewhere!

Even under the best of conditions, though, I think it would be nearly unbearable due to the condition of the roadway, which although under repair, was still as rough as a corduroy bridge. The Emperor said he would look into this situation and see that it is taken care of in a timely manner. Not much help for this trip though.

I asked why he hadn't known about this and why it was taking so long.

"It is out of my immediate jurisdiction," he said.

"But I thought you were Emperor of all the United States, which includes this great sand waste west of the city," said I.

He replied, "You are correct, Mr. Twain, and I am embarrassed to say that I am deficient in this case. The outer provinces are difficult to govern."

I couldn't tell you about the fresh perfume of flowers. The only flowers I saw were in the early portion of our movement, while still in the city. Beyond that was nothing but sand. As for their fragrance, all I could smell was the odor of wet horse blankets.

Then there was the fog. The fog became so thick we could scarcely see fifty yards in front of us, and as we approached the Cliff House, we could barely see the horse at all. We were obliged to steer by his ears, which oddly shown through the dense white mist that enveloped him. As I wrote in my article, I have no opinion of riding six miles in the clouds, but if I ever have to take another, I want to leave the horse in the stable and go in a balloon!

Once there, we could scarcely see the seals frolicking out on the rocks, let alone any sails glinting in the non-existent sunshine. Harry availed himself of a cocktail, but the Emperor and I refused – the Emperor because he didn't drink, and I because I yearned for something more effective, like a fire to warm my bones. I wrote the following:

> *We had the beach all to ourselves too, like the road. But we could not drive in the roaring surf and seem to float abroad on the foamy sea, as one is wont to do in the sunny afternoon, because the very thought of any of that icy looking water splashing on you was enough to congeal your blood, almost. We saw no white-winged ships sailing away on the billowing ocean, with the pearly light of morning descending upon them like a benediction …*

I tried out that turn of phrase on the Emperor as I reviewed what I had written.

"I admire your vocabulary," he said. "but do not be too disappointed that you cannot look out to sea. When you are unable to see what you desire, you have to imagine what it must look like."

He stood there on the beach, turned toward the sea, raised his arms, and quoted Shakespeare as was often his wont to do:

> *Behold the threaded sails,*
> *borne with the invincible and creeping wind,*
> *Draw the huge bottoms through the furrow'd sea,*
> *Breasting the lofty surge.*

If I hadn't been in a somewhat cantankerous mood at the time, I probably would have appreciated his delight and his optimism. As it was, I was dwelling more on what could have been.

But we did have each other's company. Harry drank at the bar, and I had some nice conversation with Emperor Norton. What a bright man he was. He spoke of his interest in history and literature, and I was impressed with his scientific and engineering knowledge. He even apprised me of his ideas for improvements for the railway, among other things. His only fantasy seemed to be that he was an emperor. He was convinced that he was of royal blood and that he was fulfilling his destiny to the best of his ability. Who's to argue with him? He had a royal bearing. He was a gentleman, and he truly cared for the happiness and safety of all his fellow citizens. Other than his insistence that he was Emperor, he was quite reasonable and highly intellectual. I have, much to my regret, spoken of him as a lunatic, but in reality I agree with those who regarded him as an honest, noble, intelligent man. As I said, people respected him because he respected them.

On the way back, we turned a corner too quickly and overturned the cart. Then we went on down to the steamer, where the buggy was upset again, and its axle broken. Nothing was hurt in either incident, besides our dignity. Even the Emperor took it in stride.

In my article, I wrote, *These little accidents, and all the deviltry and misfortune that preceded them, were only just and natural consequences of the absurd experiment of getting up at an hour in the morning when all God-fearing Christians ought to be in bed. I consider that the man who leaves his pillow, deliberately, at sunrise, is taking his life in his own hands and he ought to feel proud if he don't have to put it down again at the coroner's office before dark.*

*Benjamin Franklin said:*

*"Early to bed, and early to rise,
Makes a man healthy, wealthy and wise."*

*George Washington responded:*

*"I don't see it."*

 

    *Now both of these are high authorities - very high and respectable authorities – but after this morning trip to the Cliff House ... I am with General Washington first, last, and all the time on this proposition.*
    *Because I don't see it, either.*

# CHAPTER 22

Emperor Norton was making his usual rounds, inspecting the
streets and sidewalks, ensuring that none were in immediate need
of repair. Should he find some problem requiring attention, he
would be sure to bring it to the attention of someone in "his"
Public Works Department.

As he rambled down California Street, he heard a great deal
of commotion coming from around the corner. It could even be
heard above the pounding of horses' hooves on the street, and the
creaking of the cartwheels going by. When he rounded the corner,
the din became recognizable as voices raised, with scores of people
grumbling and yelling. The closer he got, the more the voices
separated into recognizable statements and slogans, especially
coming from one particular individual, standing on an inverted
barrel, so he could be seen and heard by the crowd of ruffians.

"What is this tomfoolery?" he asked of one man, who was standing back away from the crowd.

"It's a mob of intolerant people," was the reply. "They have been ranting and raving over the foreigners living and working among us – especially the Chinese. Just listen, and you'll see what I mean. They even have several Chinese men surrounded over there and won't let them leave. They're forcing them to witness their taunting."

Emperor Norton walked farther along, entering into the mob, pushing his way through them as he made his way along the sidewalk. He could now clearly hear the leader making his case to the crowd.

"They are taking our jobs! They are bringing down our wages! They are making us look bad to our employers, since they are willing to work for almost nothing. These foreigners have got to go! California is for Californians, not these low-born immigrants! Send them home where they belong!"

In 1849, when Joshua Norton arrived in San Francisco, there were fewer than 100 Chinese in the entire State of California. By this time, there were over 100,000 Chinese in California, with the lion's share in San Francisco.

Prior to 1869, and the completion of the transcontinental railroad, China was effectively closer to the California Coast than was the East Coast of the United States. This, and the fact that the Gold Rush coincided with great poverty and turmoil in Southeast China, due to the Taiping Rebellion, caused many Chinese ship captains to distribute advertising materials promoting California and its gold, calling it "Gum Saan" – Gold Mountain. Of course, they also offered their services to provide transportation across the sea, for as low as $40. Gold fever had hit the Orient, too.

The Chinese men came across the ocean to the "wild, wild east" of the American West Coast. They arrived wearing their traditional national costume: petticoat trousers down to their knees, with their lower legs wrapped in cloth stockings; thick-soled cotton shoes; large quilted jackets lined with sheepskin; and topped by large hats woven from split bamboo. Melting in with their fellow pioneers was not in the cards for these sensitive individuals.

The Chinese were an honorable people. They had a great work ethic, and a passion to do a job well. They would negotiate the best wage possible, but would take what they could get. They worked hard, were willing to learn, and provided great value as cooks, laundrymen, and servants. When times were good, they were extremely valuable employees. Not only were they welcomed, they were considered indispensable.

The tide turned, however, as the gold in the California hills thinned out and became harder to find. More and more Americans had come to California and had nearly depleted the supply. As times got more difficult, there had to be scapegoats, and in their disappointment and their bitterness, they directed their anger toward the foreigners and men of other races. The Chinese miners were forced to work older claims or to assist other miners on their claims. Eventually, legislation was passed which reserved the right of naturalization to white immigrants, making it impossible for the Chinese to own land or to file mining claims. Foreigners became less and less welcome.

The first foreigners to go were the Mexicans, the Chileans, and the French. That left the honorable Chinese to suffer from the wrath and persecution of the greedy American miners. They were easy targets. Their dark skin, their pigtails, and their unique manner of dress set them apart in a very obvious way.

Having been shunned from the gold fields, they found refuge and work in San Francisco and on the railroads. As a result, the anger began anew as the white Americans found themselves competing for jobs with these inexpensive, industrious, un-American individuals.

Times got tough. Previously, there were lots of jobs for very good pay. But as the labor pool increased in size, wages fell. Among the causes were the actions of the so-called robber barons, who found cheap labor in places like China, and brought those people over to work – especially on the new railroad. Most notable of these labor barons was the wealthy and influential Leland Stanford, whom writer Ambrose Bierce referred to as "Stealin' Landford" or (in print) "£eland $tanford".

The white workers complained that these blood-sucking creatures were taking their jobs, working happily for low wages, thus damaging the interests of the American working class. What's more, they were taking their money and sending it back to China!

It is against this background that increasing numbers of people would gather in the streets to denounce these foreigners, demanding that they get the hell out of California and leave America to the Americans.

"That is enough of this alarmingly provocative talk," shouted the Emperor. "Allow those men to go and let us all settle down."

"Who's that, then?" asked the speaker.

"I am your Emperor, Norton I, and I urge you to end this madness."

"Oh, excuse me, Your Majesty!" said the speaker, in a mocking tone. "Why don't you just send out one of your proclamations ordering us to disband. Or better yet, why don't you proclaim that these people actually be made to leave California and go back to China, and leave us to ourselves?"

"By thunder!" said Emperor Norton. "Leaving us to ourselves might be a dangerous endeavor - making us like a sinking ship with no more freight to throw overboard."

A few members of the crowd laughed.

"What would we do then?" he added. "Then we would have no

one else to blame for our troubles. You seem to have an arrogant certainty that this would solve everything."

More people in the crowd chuckled and nodded with a new understanding. "Let Emperor Norton speak. We'd like to hear his thoughts."

Bowing to increasing pressure, the speaker jumped down from atop the barrel, and several burly men lifted the Emperor up to replace him. They then stood around him to catch him should he fall, but looked more like bodyguards protecting him from the mob.

"Thank you, gentlemen," said the Emperor. "I could certainly use your services when I inspect some of the projects around the city."

Looking across the crowd, he saw that there were three Chinese men still surrounded by a group of men. "Let them go!" he shouted. "Either give them safe passage away from this crowd or, if they wish to stay, please usher them up here so they can hear what I have to say."

One of the Chinese chose to flee, the other two bravely indicated they wanted to stay near Emperor Norton. They knew he was a friend and that what he had to say would be worth hearing, even though they might not understand every word.

Emperor Norton raised his right arm pointing out to the crowd, and appeared to be preparing to make an emphatic statement. He then paused, lowered his arm, and seemed to be deep in thought. Finally, bowing his head and closing his eyes, he waited until they all fell silent, and then slowly said:

"Our Father, which art in heaven …"

Another pause. He raised his head slightly and squinted with one eye open, looking over the crowd. "Please say it with me," he said. "I am sure you know it. If I know it, you certainly must!" He then closed his eyes and, again, lowered his head. A few people joined with him, but most stayed silent:

"… hallowed be Thy name. Thy kingdom come. Thy will be done, on earth, as it is in heaven. Give us this day, our daily bread;

and forgive us our trespasses, as we forgive those who trespass against us. And lead us not into temptation, but deliver us from evil. For Thine is the kingdom, and the power, and the glory. Forever. Amen."

Emperor Norton stood there, looking out over the very silent crowd of people who stared back at him, waiting expectantly for him to say more. He raised his bowed head, and slowly straightened up, as erect as he could, giving the appearance of solidity and strength. He cleared his throat and began to speak.

"Moments ago," said the Emperor, "you told me I should send out a proclamation which would, in essence, be an Imperial edict that would bring a sudden end to this enmity I see so graphically exhibited before my eyes and ears. But you must understand that something like this, so close to our hearts, cannot be legislated. It cannot be proclaimed. It has to be a change of heart within each and every one of us as we realize that we are all of the same Creator and that we all have dreams and yearnings that such anger and division only prevent from coming into fruition."

A few bitter men didn't like what they were hearing, and quietly skulked away as he spoke.

"Are you so totally bereft of a soul? I recognize some of your faces, and I know some of your families – your dear wives who love you and depend on you – and some of your sons and daughters who look up to you for guidance. Why are you so angry?

"Even I, your beloved Emperor, have come from other shores. I may not have dark skin, or dress as they do, although some among you seem to find great entertainment in my garb, finding it somewhat peculiar.

"Can I proclaim that this all change? In no way! It has to begin within each and every one of you. I can only ask you to consider it. Some people think I am crazy, and in some ways perhaps they are right, but I am not deluded in thinking that there is an easy solution.

"We are all God's children. We all have something of value to offer each other, and in our souls, we must grapple with this division and find a solution. I do not know what that solution is, but I hope you will find a peaceful way to reach it.

"So, for now, go home. Love your family. Work hard to provide for them, but do so in a way that brings dignity to all you do. Go home, and think on these things. Do not let the fog of anger becloud this day's passing."

There was absolute silence. The people who had remained were surprisingly struck by the Emperor's eloquence. He had struck a chord, and for now, at least, they felt ashamed. Without making a sound, they all, with heads lowered, walked away.

The men who had been standing around Emperor Norton helped him down from atop the barrel. They too, wordlessly, removed themselves from his presence. He looked around, noticing that even the two Chinese gentlemen had disappeared.

Emperor Norton knew the plight of the Chinese workers in San Francisco. One of his few friends was a Chinaman, Ah How, with whom he would converse and play chess on many a pleasant afternoon in Portsmouth Square.

His words and efforts, however, fell on deaf ears. In spite of his position as Emperor he had little, if any, effect on the betterment of their status.

Despite a strong work ethic and a fierce loyalty to employers, the Chinese workers in California never abandoned an abiding love for their homeland. In fact, for many years, they chose to be buried in the land of their birth. As a result, many "death ships" made their way westward across the Pacific Ocean from San Francisco carrying Chinese corpses back to their native soil.

Due to the restrictive laws in the State of California aimed at keeping the Chinese workers "in their place", which persists even now, in 1880, they have never been allowed to settle in.

I must tell you that I, too, paid a price in all this trouble. It was the practice of my newspaper, the *Daily Morning Call*, to use the derogatory term, "Mongolians", when referring to the Chinese people in San Francisco. I objected strongly to that. In spite of my bully pulpit as a reporter, and writing a daily column, I was unable to prevail. I was eventually fired from the newspaper when I started writing articles critical of the treatment of the Chinese by hateful hoodlums, and of the police officers' apathetic disregard for such behavior.

These people could have learned a lot from the gentle soul of Emperor Norton!

# CHAPTER 23

A fine spring morning bestowed itself upon the City of San Francisco. What little fog there had been in the early hours had vanished, revealing a warm sun rising into a clear, blue sky.

Moving down the street, his walking stick clicking once with every two steps he took, Freddie Coombs walked erect, even though he was weighted down on one side. His left arm was wrapped around a thick pile of placards and his left hand tightly gripped a large heavy mallet. He ignored the men who passed, but as he was able, he bowed slightly to any lady – of whatever repute – who went by. Ordinarily he would have tipped his tri-cornered hat, but with his present cargo, that was not possible.

Freddie Coombs, thanks to his constant efforts at self-promotion was also known as George Washington II. Professionally a phrenologist, he earned his keep analyzing the bumps on people's heads. His analysis of their craniums gave him insights into their intelligence and wisdom. Of course, paying customers were always given positive results.

Freddie Coombs, in reality, held much in common with Emperor Norton – although neither man would be caught dead admitting it. Highly intelligent, he was an inventor. He invented a ditch-digging machine for use on farms. He developed a train propulsion system using electromagnetism. And, in a case of bad timing, he built a working telegraph in 1840, only to be bested by Samuel Morse who successfully obtained the patent.

He loved to be known and acknowledged as his alter ego: the reincarnation of George Washington, the Father of the Country.

There was, indeed, a great resemblance between the two, especially when Freddie would don the hat, the knee breaches and his powdered wig. Often he would be seen carrying a banner proclaiming that "the Spirit of Washington still lives!" He also put himself forward as "The Great Matrimonial Candidate", as he was actively searching for a woman who might consider becoming his "Martha".

On this day, his mood was less than jovial. He had a bone to pick with Emperor Norton, that lunatic who roamed the streets. Freddie was out distributing posters advertising his services when he came upon a street corner where some of his posters, previously hung, had been taken down. From the evidence, they had not just been removed, they had been viciously torn from the walls so that the ragged corners remained nailed to the surface. Malfeasance was patently obvious.

Coombs decided to suspend his marketing efforts long enough to go to the police to report the vandalism. He knew who the culprit was. It was that damnable Emperor Norton.

Officer William Martin told Freddie Coombs that it was not a criminal offense to remove posters, so there was nothing he could do for him. Officer Martin suggested that he might want to file a civil suit against Emperor Norton.

Too much trouble and too much expense was Freddie's conclusion, so he went to the editor of the *Alta California* newspaper, Frederick MacCrellish – my old boss - demanding that he place an article warning the Emperor to cease and desist.

"Why do you suspect the Emperor?" asked MacCrellish.

"Because he is jealous of my reputation with the ladies," was the answer.

Frederick MacCrellish refused to print such an article.

Something must have been in the air that day, as Emperor Norton was in a similar state of unhappiness. During his usual rounds, he had noticed many of Freddie Coombs' posters placed in what he considered to be unlawful places. They cluttered up the area and degraded its ambiance. What's more, some of them had been placed in locations that covered up his own royal warrants.

Emperor Norton was scandalized to think that George Washington II, that lunatic, would do such a thing. As the newspapers were generally supportive of his efforts and published his proclamations, he decided to take his beef to the *Alta California*.

No sooner had Freddie Coombs stormed out the door and vacated the area, when Emperor Norton stomped into the building. MacCrellish, not able to see around the corner, heard the familiar sound of a walking stick on the wood floor and he thought Freddie Coombs had returned.

"I told you no!" he yelled through the office door.

"I beg your pardon?" said the Emperor.

Realizing his mistake, MacCrellish apologized and asked what he could do.

"I want a notice put in the paper that it is illegal to put up posters in certain areas of the city, and I want George Washington II put on notice that it will not be tolerated."

Even the Emperor's demands were not acted upon immediately. Instead, the *Alta California* published an article comparing Emperor Norton and George Washington II. They noted the Emperor's slovenliness but minimized his delusion, while they emphasized the apparent insanity of George Washington II.

George Washington II was mortified to read that he was

considered insane, but even more so because it was unthinkable that he would be compared in any way to the true lunatic.

Ultimately, Emperor Norton submitted a proclamation which was published. *"The Chief of Police is hereby ordered to seize upon the person of Professor Coombs, falsely called Washington No. 2, as a seditious and turbulent fellow, and to have him sent forthwith, for his own and the public good, to the State Lunatic Asylum for at least thirty days!"*

Freddie Coombs folded. Although he would never admit it, he knew he lacked the charm and the diplomacy that Emperor Norton held in spades. He realized he could never be successful challenging the Emperor's authority, so he eventually packed up and hightailed himself back to New York, the city of his origin.

Sometimes I wonder if, perhaps, Freddie Coombs was more sane than he was given credit for. In this case, at least, he saw the difference between himself and the Emperor, and did what was probably the best thing he could have done under the circumstances.

By the way, I ran into him much later. He was, indeed, back in New York – and up to his old shenanigans. He was trying to collect on a bill he submitted to the U.S. Congress in the amount of 17 quadrillion dollars in payment for expenses he had incurred while working for the well-being of the country. When the William Penn mansion in Philadelphia was due for demolition, Coombs asked the U.S. Congress to give it to him. Eventually, it was torn down, whereupon he changed his demand, asking instead for the more-fitting Washington Monument.

From the far reaches of the country had come another pretender to the throne. An article in the *Alta California* announced his accession:

### Another Emperor in the Field

*Since the advent of Maximilian we are having a heavy run of Kings, Emperors, and similar humbugs, and the disease threatens to become an epidemic in*

> *America. We would respectfully call the attention
> of our beloved Emperor, Norton I, to the case of a
> blackguard in New York who styles himself "Stellifer
> the King, Reigning Prince of the House of David and
> Guardian of American Destinies." This fellow, who
> appears to be a man of some education and luxurious
> tastes, has been boarding at all the leading hotels in
> Boston, New York and Saratoga, and other places,
> and when dunned for his bills agrees to settle when
> his stake of $3,500,000 was paid by the United
> States Treasury.*

This blackguard of whom they spoke was D. Stellifer Moulton, a newspaper correspondent who, obviously went off the deep end, lost his job and his credibility. He decided he needed to start his own newspaper in order to effectively advocate for his crazy ideas, so he demanded that the leading newspapermen of the time each donate a half million dollars to his endeavor.

In the meantime, his expensive tastes got him into trouble. He would check into top-notch hotels and sign the bills as "Stellifer the King", telling the management that they could charge his expenses to the U.S. Treasury (sound familiar?). Needless to say, D. Stellifer Moulton was subsequently apprehended by the authorities and ended up in the lunatic asylum on Blackwell's Island. Another imposter put away, and another victory for Emperor Norton.

The Emperor's reign was not without other bumps in the road and included challenges from a few of his own subjects. Even though he was rather well known, especially in the tourism industry, and instantly recognizable to many visitors to the city, there were a few people still ignorant as to his status and his identity.

One of these challenges came from the Central Pacific Railroad, the very railroad he had supported and inspected – even though the railroad president, Mr. Leland Stanford himself, had given the Emperor carte blanche access to passage on the rails.

On one of his trips from San Francisco to Sacramento, in order to sit in at the California Assembly, as was his custom, he was challenged by a conductor on the line who demanded a ticket from the Emperor.

"But I do not need one!" the Emperor said.

"Everybody needs a ticket," replied the conductor.

"But I am Emperor Norton, and I am allowed to travel anywhere without the burden of a ticket."

"A burden? A ticket isn't a burden; it's what gives you the right to travel on this train."

"What I am trying to say is that owing to my position, my loyal friend, Mr. Leland Stanford, has afforded me the privilege of unlimited travel on the line."

"Do you have a ticket or letter indicating such?"

"No, sir, I do not. I think just the fact that I am the Emperor and am wearing my ceremonial uniform is enough. I am on an official junket to Sacramento as guest of the Legislature. I demand you correct this oversight."

After much ballyhoo, the problem was resolved, only to be revisited when the Emperor headed to the dining car for a free meal.

In a related incident, the Emperor was once ordered off a riverboat for not paying his fare. Needless to say, he was indignant, and upon his return to the royal library, he officially ordered that the U.S. Navy blockade all of that particular company's vessels. His threat worked, and the board of directors sent an apology and a free lifetime pass.

Incidents such as these were not common, but acted as occasional irritants to an otherwise happy rule.

# CHAPTER 24

There were two dogs that drove Emperor Norton to distraction. He hated the dogs, even though they liked him and often followed him on his rounds. His dislike for them was magnified when he was linked to them, as though they were his loyal and desired companions. If anyone dared intimate that they were his own personal pets, he would fly off the handle. In spite of this, Bummer and Lazarus were important working dogs in the City of San Francisco and were of great interest to the people and the journalists of the city. These dogs carried on the very important tradition of killing rats.

At one time, life was so slow in Yerba Buena that there wasn't much of interest to the scant native rat population. According to the old timers, an occasional lazy rat might saunter across the plaza but did no damage. As the village grew into the City of San Francisco, and with the influx of gold seekers, mainly from across the seas, the rat population grew and diversified. By the early 1850's, vessels from countless other ports brought every variety of rat – every size, every shape, and every color. Most were quite large, and they did lots of damage to the wares and goods handled by the merchants and store keepers. Cats had been "imported" from Southern California, but faced with angry rats, as large, or larger, than they were, it wasn't long before the cats refused to work and went on strike.

Later, an English Terrier named Tips was brought in. It was said that Tips' sole delight was to hunt out and destroy rats. In pursuance of this interesting occupation, he would, as once written, "neglect food, friends, shelter, and all the comforts of dog-life, simply repaid if he succeeded in digging out from his hole some one of the rat tribe, the mortal enemy of his race". Tips was so successful that, soon, other dogs were brought in for the purpose of policing the streets and doing their best to rid the town of the growing rodent population.

Two such dogs were Bummer and Lazarus. Bummer was a medium-sized, shaggy-haired, black dog of questionable pedigree, who was well known for his heroic efforts in the killing of rats as he regularly patrolled up and down Montgomery Street. Lazarus was a small, yellow, short-haired brute, equally of questionable pedigree. It was believed that one day Bummer rescued Lazarus from a fight and ever since that day Lazarus followed Bummer wherever he went. They began working in tandem and terrorized the rat population in a way that it had never before experienced. In one celebrated mission, they killed 85 rats in only 20 minutes.

The dogs seemed to know how to ingratiate themselves with people and made themselves extremely useful by parlaying their talent for chasing rats and their personal delight in killing them. Storekeepers found them of such great value that to have either Bummer or Lazarus rid their shops from the plague of rats, the publicity they gained would be a boon to their business. The dogs' efforts became quite newsworthy and the two canines benefited additionally from the treats brought to them by reporters looking for a story. Editors of the *Californian*, the *Daily Alta California*, the *Daily Morning Call*, and the *Evening Bulletin* all vied for stories about the dogs.

When Bummer was shot in the leg, and put temporarily out of commission, Lazarus left him to work with another dog. Readers were upset. But when Bummer recovered, and Lazarus returned to his side, the readers cheered. It was a canine drama, covered in the daily newspapers.

At the height of Bummer's and Lazarus' popularity came Edward Jump, an out-of-work artist and cartoonist who began to get some work supplying the local newspapers with caricatures of some of the characters who entertained the local population: George Washington the Second, The King of Pain and others whom the City of San Francisco had embraced. Among his subjects were Emperor Norton – and Bummer and Lazarus. The fiction of the two dogs belonging to the Emperor was magnified, when Jump published a cartoon titled "The Three Bummers" which showed Emperor Norton grazing at a buffet table with the two dogs at his feet begging for scraps.

One unfortunate shopkeeper displayed the cartoon in his window. On passing, Emperor Norton saw it and became so angry that he shattered the shop window by slamming it with his walking stick.

Lazarus left this mortal coil in late 1863. The newspaper reported that he had been kicked by one of the horses pulling a fire engine down the street. It later came out that he was actually poisoned by a piece of meat laced with "rat bane" after he reportedly bit a young boy. Edward Jump produced a cartoon for publication in the newspaper depicting Lazarus' funeral. In it he depicted Emperor Norton as the Pope performing the funeral ceremony, and George Washington the Second digging the grave. In actuality, Lazarus was not buried – he was sent to a taxidermist, stuffed, and displayed behind the bar in Frederick Martin's saloon.

In the July 31, 1864 issue of the *Daily Morning Call*, following the death of Lazarus, I wrote about these dogs:

*The lamented Lazarus departed this life about a year ago, and from that time until recently poor Bummer has mourned the life of his faithful friend in solitude, scorning the sympathy and companionship of his race with that stately reserve and exclusiveness which has always distinguished him since he became a citizen of San Francisco. But, for several weeks past, we have observed a vagrant black puppy has taken up with him, and attends him in his promenades, bums with him at the restaurants, and watches over his slumbers as unremittingly as did the sainted Lazarus of other days. Whether that puppy really feels an unselfish affection for Bummer, or whether he is actuated by unworthy motives, and goes with him merely to ring in on the eating houses through his popularity at such establishments, or whether, he is one of those fawning sycophants that fasten upon the world's heroes in order that they may be glorified by the reflected light of greatness, we cannot yet determine. We only know that he hangs around Bummer, and snarls at intruders upon his repose, and looks proud and happy when the old dog condescends to notice him. He ventures upon no puppyish levity in the presence of his prince, and essays no unbecoming familiarity, but in all respects conducts himself with respectful decorum which such a puppy so situated should display. Consequently, in time, he may grow into high favor.*

It is not known what happened with Bummer and the faithful black puppy. After the death of Lazarus, Bummer's star had fallen and the people and reporters of San Francisco lost interest. Bummer met his maker in late 1865. His death did not make the headlines as did that of Lazarus, but I wrote his eulogy. Here's what I said:

*The old vagrant 'Bummer' is really dead at last; and although he was always more respected than his obsequious vassal, the dog 'Lazarus,' his exit has not made half as much stir in the newspaper world as did the departure of the latter. I think it is because he died a natural death: died with friends around him to smooth his pillow and wipe the death-damps from his brow, and receive his last words of love and resignation; because he died full of years, and honor, and disease, and fleas. He was permitted to die a natural death, as I have said, but poor Lazarus 'died with his boots on' - which is to say, he lost his life by violence; he gave up the ghost mysteriously, at dead of night, with none to cheer his last moments or soothe his dying pains. So the murdered dog was canonized in the newspapers, his shortcomings excused and his virtues heralded to the world; but his superior, parting with his life in the fullness of time, and in the due course of nature, sinks as quietly as might the mangiest cur among us. Well, let him go. In earlier days he was courted and caressed; but latterly he has lost his comeliness - his dignity had given place to a want of self-respect, which allowed him to practice mean deceptions to regain for a moment that sympathy and notice which had become necessary to his very existence, and it was evident to all that the dog had had his day; his great popularity was gone forever. In fact, Bummer should have died sooner: there was a time when his death would have left a lasting legacy of fame to his name. Now, however, he will be forgotten in a few days. Bummer's skin is to be stuffed and placed with that of Lazarus.*

Bummer was, indeed, sent to the taxidermist, and is displayed alongside his former associate. Edward Jump produced yet another cartoon. He memorialized Bummer by showing him lying in state with Lazarus in heaven above him, dining from a table filled with food. Surrounding the bier are several rats paying their respects. The caption referred to the two dogs as "The Damon and Pythias of San Francisco", calling upon the Greek legend which personified trust, loyalty, and true friendship.

# CHAPTER 25

Emperor Norton returned to the boarding house from one of his sorties around the city. He mounted the stairway, his walking stick thumping each step as he went up, and his saber, strapped at his side, occasionally scraping against the wall. As his walk had been an official one, he was dressed in his ceremonial uniform with the rumpled, faded military jacket with tarnished gold epaulets, a Kossuth hat with gold cord and an ostrich plume, plus his noisy, clanking accoutrements.

At the top of the flight of stairs, on the second floor, he encountered his landlord talking with a gentleman, apparently about his interest in the vacant room at the closer end of the hallway.

"Good afternoon, Your Highness," said the landlord.

"Good day, sir," said Norton, giving a nod of greeting to the visitor.

The Emperor paused, removed his hat, and wiped his sweaty brow with a bright red silk cloth taken from his pocket. As he did so, a sudden surprised look of recognition lit up the visitor's face.

"My goodness!" He exclaimed. "Are you not Joshua Norton?"

"Well, ah, yes ..." said the Emperor, haltingly. "My name is Norton."

"I'm Nathan Peiser," said the visitor. "Do you remember me from many years ago? In South Africa?"

"Oh, my goodness, that was some time ago, indeed."

The landlord quietly slipped away, allowing the two men to visit. It sounded as though they had some catching up to do. He was sure he could talk with the man named Peiser before he left.

"Nathan Peiser, you say?" asked Emperor Norton. "You may have to remind me how we know each other."

"Well, sir, it was back in '42. I was on the crew of the ship, *Waterloo*. We were on our way from London to Australia, transporting a large number of convicts to Botany Bay. We had put into Cape Town, in August it was, as we were very low on water. While at anchor in Table Bay, a terrible north-easter swept through causing the Waterloo to lose anchor and go aground on a reef, where it was dashed to pieces on the rocks."

"How terrible," said Norton. "I think I vaguely recollect something to that effect."

"Yes sir, Joshua," said Nathan Peiser. "Almost two hundred men died that day, and many others were greatly injured. I was one of the fortunate survivors, although badly hurt. I was sent to the English hospital in Cape Town. There were quite a few merchants of Jewish extraction in town, and a certain John Norton, who had a ship chandlery store, was one of them. They came to the hospital fearing that some of their friends were among the injured. Since I was a Jew, I attracted his attention and we formed an acquaintance. As it happened, I knew his brother and some of his friends back in London."

"Is that so!" said Emperor Norton. He was slowly beginning to remember.

"Can you believe it?" said Nathan Peiser. "In any event, as I convalesced, he took me to his home and introduced me to his wife and children – you, of course, being among them. I believe you were in your late twenties at the time."

"I would have been 24 or 25."

"Yes, that sounds about right. At your home, your father led Jewish prayers quite often, and as I recall, that was the source of some amusement for you. You didn't seem to share his deep faith. I even remember one day when you were severely reprimanded for provoking your father!"

Suddenly, in a flash of recognition, Norton exclaimed, "Why, yes, Nathan, now I distinctly remember you, and the correction I received for raising a disturbance at that Jewish prayer meeting!"

Norton was grimacing inwardly, not really enjoying this reminder of the past. This little man was dredging up some of what he had struggled with during his wilderness years and what he had wanted to put well behind himself. However, in true royal fashion, he was polite and patient, and showed grace under increasing pressure.

In keeping with that spirit, Norton graciously invited Nathan Peiser up to his room on the third floor. He was determined to be hospitable, but would make the visit as short as possible. They mounted the last flight of stairs, with the Emperor's walking stick thumping on every step, and his scepter scraping against the wall, adding one more scratch to the many already there. Showing his guest into his room, Norton motioned for him to sit on the only chair in the room, as the Emperor removed his scepter and his hat. He placed his walking stick in the corner among a large collection of other walking sticks already leaning against the wall. Then he took a seat on the small bed.

"So tell me, what brings you to San Francisco?" asked Emperor Norton, not really interested, but still a bit shocked by this coincidental meeting.

"I'm a tailor now. I have been for many years. After leaving Cape Town, I went to Germany and learned how to sew and repair clothing. Eventually, I made my way to the United States and worked back east for some time. When the war came along, I enlisted and fought for the Union. I was lucky enough to make it through with only minor injuries. I took up tailoring again once the war ended. Now I've come out west, looking for a new start in California. Isn't it fortuitous that I just happened to be looking for temporary lodging today, and chose this time to visit your building!"

"Yes, yes, fortuitous indeed," answered Norton, trying very hard to sound pleased.

After sharing a few other memories, many of which Norton had conveniently forgotten, Nathan Peiser asked, "How is it that you came by the title of Emperor? And why do you wear such a uniform as this?"

Norton's demeanor changed suddenly, as he got up from the bed, went to the door, and turned the key, locking it with a click. He went back to Nathan Peiser, who was still seated on the chair, and leaned down, bending close to his ear, as though he were going to divulge a very great secret.

"I am about to tell you something that you must never repeat to another soul. It has to do with my family and my youth in Cape Town."

"Well, yes, I promise."

"It is important you understand the following: John Norton was not my real father. I am, in fact, a crown prince to the throne of France, and I was sent to Cape Town with the Norton family in order to protect me from assassination."

"Is this true, or are you having fun at my expense?" asked Nathan Peiser.

"This is deadly serious, my friend. I was adopted by John

Norton and his wife. I very much appreciated what they were willing to do for me, and I still honor their efforts on my behalf by keeping their name. I took the title of "Emperor" because I am legally and rightly entitled to it. Therefore I am Emperor Norton, and am called such by all of my subjects in the United States."

Nathan Peiser had a very quizzical look on his face.

"You look troubled, my friend," said Norton. He continued, "The uniform, which you have asked about, was given to me by Queen Victoria. She delivered it to me, personally, in appreciation of the fine job I have been doing here in the United States."

"But, she's English! And you're a South African Jew claiming to be of French royalty! Why would she do that?" asked Nathan Peiser.

Emperor Norton didn't answer. He just glared at the intruder.

By this time, Nathan Peiser was squirming in his chair and quizzically looking at Norton, obviously not believing a word of what he was saying.

"Forgive me for saying this, Joshua, but this just doesn't add up. Frankly, I think you're crazy!"

Nathan Peiser froze. He wasn't accustomed to speaking his mind quite so forthrightly, especially in such a negative manner. "What are you doing?" he asked himself. "Did you just call him crazy?!"

There was a long pause. Norton looked at Nathan Peiser, then away, then back. In a lowered voice, with a tone of resignation, he merely said, "And so do a good many others." He then just stared into Mr. Peiser's eyes, waiting for him to flinch.

He flinched.

"Well, this has been very interesting," said Nathan Peiser, "but I really must go and find suitable lodgings before the end of the day."

"You mean you do not like it here?" asked Emperor Norton, hoping for a negative response.

"No, I believe the rooms are too small for me ..."

Norton breathed a quick sigh of relief.

"... so I'll be looking at a few other places."

Norton didn't want to impede his exit, so he stood, went to the door, and unlocked it as quickly as possible. "What a delightful surprise," he said as he moved to the side allowing Nathan Peiser to go out. "May you have a beautiful life here in California."

"Thank you, Joshua," said Nathan Peiser, refusing to acknowledge him as his Imperial Majesty or any such thing. "Best wishes to you!"

They parted, both being left with a very uncomfortable feeling, and both not really hoping their paths would ever cross again.

For Emperor Norton this was a rather unpleasant, but at the same time a very significant event. While bringing up those memories he had previously grappled with and sought to forget, this chance encounter forced him to deal with them one more time. It was like when a reformed alcoholic comes across a bottle of liquor and rather than let it draw him back into his trouble, he has the fortitude to pour it out and not let it destroy him. To most people, this would not have been a challenge, but for Norton, it was an important testing. He had come through it in good form, and he didn't let it get him down. This visit with Nathan Peiser even helped steel him and prepare him for the next challenge he was about to face.

It was only a few months later when the local authorities forced him to defend his sanity in a very big way.

# CHAPTER 26

On the morning of January 21, 1867, there occurred a civic calamity of major proportions. A rookie cop arrested the Emperor of the United States. Young, overly-zealous local patrolman, Officer Armand Barbier, was summoned by the proprietor of the Palace Hotel to remove a shabby-looking gentleman from his premises.

The gentleman in question was, of course, Emperor Norton. He was, at the time, in the seventh year of his benevolent reign. During these years of service to his people, all he demanded in return was a little civility, and a little respect. On this morning, all he wanted was a little peace and quiet.

Emperor Norton was merely exercising one of his daily routines of finding a comfortable chair in which to place his royal personage as he read the latest newspaper. His usual location of choice was the favored Empire House Hotel, situated close to his lodgings. Unfortunately for him, on this morning, his schedule required adjustment, as the lobby of the Empire House was undergoing some painting and minor renovation. Ordinarily, this would have been a major inconvenience for the Emperor, but as he was in a particularly accepting mood he looked upon this as an opportunity to try something new. As a result, he chose the lobby of the Palace Hotel for his morning reading. He even liked the name of the hotel, as it equally suited his status. If the Empire is temporarily not available, he reasoned, one could do much worse than the Palace.

Norton was dressed in his usual "finery". He wore his scruffy pale blue army uniform with brass buttons and tarnished, gold-plated epaulettes, and his tattered old boots with slits on the sides to accommodate the corns on his feet. His black beaver hat with its bright white plume of ostrich feathers sat on the table in front of him, and his carved-serpent walking stick leaned against the side of his chair. In anticipation of a possible rainstorm later in the day, he also had at his side his favorite lacquered Chinese umbrella.

Suddenly, the silence he enjoyed was shattered by a loud voice which began from across the lobby and approached in the form of the stuffy hotel manager.

"Off you go!" shouted Mr. Oliver Lonsdale. "You'll have to leave the premises."

"I beg your pardon," protested Emperor Norton. "You are telling me to leave?"

"That's exactly right. You are obviously not a guest at this hotel and you are not welcome here."

"But …"

"No buts. No excuses. I am telling you that you must go. Now!"

"Do you know to whom you are speaking in this most intemperate manner?"

"I am talking to someone who does not belong here," said the proprietor. "And yes, I do know who you are. I have seen you walking the streets, and I know you have a certain following among some people, but your rights do not extend to the lobby of this hotel unless you are a paying guest."

Mr. Lonsdale knew that his small hotel was not among the finest in the city (It is not to be confused with the later, larger, and much more lavish Palace Hotel which replaced it). While not totally fulfilling the promise of its name, the Palace Hotel afforded modest comfort at reasonable rates. Mr. Lonsdale felt that a nice atmosphere and good service made up for a lot and he worked diligently to give his hostelry a modicum of class. Having purchased the building and investing money, sweat and time creating its success, he took matters very seriously and avidly defended the hotel's reputation. The presence of the likes of Emperor Norton, he felt, did not meet his aesthetic sense, nor did it contribute to the ambiance for which he strove. His desire to expel the Emperor from his establishment overrode his common sense and blinded his eyes to the fact that his intentions, handled in this manner, could have serious social repercussions.

"Then you do know," Norton said, "that you are talking to Norton I, Emperor of the United States of America, and if anyone is able to add a bit of class to your establishment, it is I. You should be pleased to have me here, and would do well to value my patronage."

"Patronage? That's a laugh!" said Mr. Lonsdale. "Class? That, too, is a misplaced concept. Get out or I call the police!"

"I might consider moving on if I receive an apology for your rudeness."

Again, Mr. Lonsdale spoke before thinking. "Not a chance. You should apologize to me for taking up space in my hotel, and for wasting my time in dealing with you."

"You are very rude, sir. I will not leave without an apology."

"We'll see about that!" said Mr. Lonsdale. He stood, paused, and looked at Emperor Norton with strident contempt. Again, his anger got the better of him. He turned his back and purposefully stomped across the lobby and into his office behind the desk.

It was then that Officer Barbier was summoned.

Officer Barbier's enthusiasm stemmed not only from his youth – he was 19 – but also from the fact that he was a "local" – one of 66 uniformed "special officers" who had been hired by the beleaguered Chief of Police, Patrick Crowley, to supplement the small regular force of policemen on duty. Anxious to express his authority and find someone committing an infraction, he was elated to have been called.

Officer Barbier burst into the lobby as though he was on his way to a fire. He had been apprised of his mission and this was his first such call in his very new career. He wanted to make the most of it.

Not seeing Emperor Norton ensconced in his chair behind a giant split-leaf philodendron, he rushed over to a solitary gentleman sitting in another over-stuffed chair near the center of the lobby. It happened to be Mr. John Butler, a visiting lumberman from Portland, Oregon – a paying guest at the Palace Hotel. It was Mr. Butler's misfortune to be the first gentleman in Officer Barbier's line of sight.

"Excuse me sir, but you can't be here," cautioned Officer Barbier. "This is a private establishment."

"I beg your pardon, Officer," said Mr. Butler, startled by his abrupt presence. Barbier stood so close that Mr. Butler had to look almost straight up.

"You are trespassing, sir, and you'll have to leave."

"How can I be trespassing, when I am staying here?" protested Mr. Butler.

"Staying here?" sputtered Officer Barbier. "You mean you are a guest here?"

Just then Mr. Lonsdale noticed the mistake and came rushing over to correct the situation.

"One moment, officer. I'm afraid you have the wrong man," said Mr. Lonsdale.

"Oh, I beg your pardon", said Officer Barbier, bowing to the guest.

"The interloper is over there," said Mr. Lonsdale. He pointed to Emperor Norton who was watching intently and laughing at the sideshow.

Officer Barbier stepped over to Emperor Norton while Mr. Lonsdale remained behind to smooth the ruffled feathers of his paying guest.

"Excuse me sir, but you can't be here," cautioned Officer Barbier. "This is a private establishment."

"Yes," replied Norton, laughing. "I heard you tell that to the other man. Thank you for explaining that to me, too, but I am merely sitting here reading a newspaper." Norton looked to his right and then to his left. Shrugging his shoulders, he said, "No one else has had need of this chair."

"That's not the issue, sir. You are not a paying customer - as is that gentleman, I might add." Barbier pointed across the lobby to Mr. Butler who still appeared indignant despite Mr. Lonsdale's frantic public relations efforts.

"But you do not understand, officer. I am allowed to go anywhere I want. In fact, most places encourage my presence as it greatly helps their business to have my patronage and support."

"Well, sir, I think I have heard enough. Obviously, such is not the case in this establishment. Based on the complaint lodged, I'm going to have to arrest you and take you to jail."

"I beg your pardon?" protested Emperor Norton. "Arrest me? For what charge?"

"Since you certainly don't belong here, and judging from your manner of dress, I am charging you with vagrancy."

"Vagrancy?"

"Yes. It's the crime of idleness, with no visible means of support and no place to call home."

"I know what vagrancy is!" said Norton. "But I cannot believe you are arresting me for it!"

"There, there. That's enough. That's all I want to hear from you. Come along."

"But I am no vagrant! I am the Emperor of the United States!"

"Okay. That really is the limit! No more from you, or I'll add insanity to the charge."

"Officer, I will respect your position and, in fact, I respect your concern for the public welfare, but in this case you are very wrong, indeed. Perhaps I may speak with your superior."

"Oh, yes, you will certainly have that opportunity. In just a few moments you can speak with the desk sergeant on duty."

Emperor Norton knew that, at this point, resisting the officer would lead to further embarrassment and a certain loss of dignity.

"Okay, Officer, let us go and settle this with your Sergeant. I assume that, owing to his rank, he will have a bit more common sense."

Wisely, and quite out of character, the impulsive Officer Barbier let the comment go without a retort. "That's fine sir. Let's go."

Officer Barbier reached for his handcuffs.

"I forbid you to use those manacles on me!" said Emperor Norton with as much regal indignity as he could muster.

Barbier quickly succumbed to the Emperor's protest. He took hold of Emperor Norton's arm and led him out of the Palace Hotel and down the street toward the precinct headquarters.

They arrived at the door. Officer Barbier opened it and ushered Emperor Norton into the building.

"Thank you, officer, you are very kind," said the Emperor. After all, he was not an unreasonable monarch. He recognized and appreciated proper respect.

Barbier led him up to the desk, where the sergeant was shuffling some paperwork. Looking up, the sergeant said, "What have we got here, Barbier?"

"Sir, I have arrested this man on charges of vagrancy. He was trespassing in the lobby of the Palace Hotel. He was asked, by the manager, to leave and refused to do so when I confronted him."

"All I wanted was an apology from that very rude man at the

hotel!" said the Emperor. "And I was not trespassing. I was merely sitting there reading a newspaper."

"But a charge of vagrancy does not depend on that," said the sergeant. "It means you are shiftless or idle and that you are wandering around without money or work."

"Yes, I know what it means," said Norton, quite tired of going around in all these circles. "The problem is that it is not true. Firstly, I am not a vagrant. I am Norton I, Emperor of the United States. Secondly, I have here in this pocket, let me see …"

He took some money out of his pocket. "Four dollars, no, four dollars and 75 cents. In legal tender. So I am not without means."

The sergeant winced.

Norton reached into another pocket. "And here I have a key. This is the key to my residence at the Eureka Lodgings, 624 Commercial Street here in the city. So I am not without a home. How can I be considered a vagrant?"

The sergeant winced again.

"The gentleman does have a point, Officer Barbier. Actually two good points. I would discount the Emperor business, however. That's obviously a tough one to swallow. But I've seen him out on the street occasionally and he doesn't seem to offer any danger to anyone. Did you not properly determine his status?"

"Well, um, I …" Barbier sputtered.

The desk sergeant continued, "It seems pretty clear that he does have money and a residence. I realize he should have been more responsive to the hotel manager, but I would, indeed, have a hard time booking him in for vagrancy. In fact, that's not going to happen."

"Well, what about that Emperor business?" asked Barbier, whose credibility was about to be destroyed. He had to save his reputation. "You heard him. He says he is Emperor of the United States and, on the way down here, he told me that the Mayor and all the city employees work for him! He also claims that the California Legislature takes counsel from him, and the

United States Congress receives instructions from him. If he's not a vagrant, he is most assuredly crazy! So, I am arresting him for the crime of lunacy."

"Lunacy, Officer Barbier? As in crazy? Insane?"

"Yes, sir."

"Now you have really gone overboard," said Emperor Norton. "I have money. Not much, but enough to qualify for having means. And I have a home, modest as it might be. And, I have a job – well, a position actually – as Emperor of these United States, to which I was elevated at the request of my loyal subjects."

"There, you see, sir," said Officer Barbier. "If he isn't a lunatic I don't know what he is."

"Do you insist on pressing charges of lunacy against this man, officer?" asked the desk sergeant.

"I do, indeed."

"Then I will have to book him into the jail overnight and notify Mr. Wingate Jones. We will have to let the law take its proper course."

"Who is Mr. Wingate Jones?" asked Emperor Norton.

"He's the Commissioner of Lunacy for the City of San Francisco," replied the desk sergeant.

"This is an outrage!" shouted the Emperor. "You gentlemen are making a very big mistake. I will see that it is corrected and you are admonished for this."

In spite of his protestations, Emperor Norton was booked into jail for the night.

He was tired after all this hullabaloo and since the jail cell was about the same size as his room at the lodging house, he didn't feel all that uncomfortable. It did lack all the familiar accoutrements, but he was determined to make the best of a bad situation, knowing that it would all be set straight in the morning.

His walking stick and umbrella had been taken from him, but he had his boots, which he carefully removed, placing them under the cot; and his beloved beaver hat (with ostrich feather and rosette), which he ceremoniously placed in the safest place he could find, which was on the cot next to the cold cement wall. He then settled in for a sleepless night.

The news got out, though, thanks to an enterprising reporter who had come to check on the day's activities at the police station. Recognizing the name of the celebrity prisoner (the sergeant, ironically, had recorded his name as "Emperor Norton"), he couldn't resist that story. The news spread quickly. Knowing that the people of the city would go wild over the news of this calamity, the newspapers ran with it.

Most notable was The *Evening Bulletin* which wrote:

> *In what can only be described as the most dastardly of errors, Joshua A. Norton was arrested today. He is being held on the ludicrous charge of 'Lunacy'. Known and loved by all true San Franciscans as Emperor Norton, this kindly Monarch of Montgomery Street is less a lunatic than those who have engineered these trumped up charges. As they will learn, His Majesty's loyal subjects are fully apprised of this outrage. Perhaps a return to the methods of the Vigilance Committees is in order.*

> *"This newspaper urges all right-thinking citizens to be in attendance tomorrow at the public hearing to be held before the Commissioner of Lunacy, Wingate Jones. The blot on the record of San Francisco must be removed.*

The stage was set. A showdown was imminent. The commissioner and the chief of police were put on alert.

# CHAPTER 27

Mr. Wingate Jones did not sleep well that night. The Norton hearing had been scheduled for 10 o'clock the following morning, and he didn't feel it should take place at all. He had rehearsed his reasons all night, running them over and over through his head and was ready to state his case to Chief of Police Patrick Crowley first thing in the morning.

He crept out of bed early and allowed his wife to prepare a good morning meal. In spite of his agitation, he couldn't let a good breakfast go to waste.

Mr. Wingate Jones was a corpulent individual, slow-moving, and obviously, at the age of 62, beyond his prime. His formerly youthful body had given way to his love affair with the dinner table (the breakfast and lunch table as well), and the years had taken their toll. Contrary to the custom of the time, he had no facial hair – not even a mustache. The few strands of hair on top of his head were combed over in a vain attempt to cover the bald spot. He looked much like Dickens' Mr. Pickwick with his round, chinless face, squinting through his tiny, round spectacles.

He found his way to Crowley's office in the city hall, arriving just after seven o'clock. As the chief was not there yet, Mr. Wingate Jones paced the hallway, anxiously taking out his pocket watch every few minutes and coming by the office door hoping to see or hear Chief Crowley.

Mr. Wingate Jones had held lunacy hearings countless times during his long career. Almost without exception, previous hearings had been quiet, somber affairs involving the individual whose sanity was in question, some medical personnel and, perhaps, a few family members. Experience taught him that in such situations the medical people sought to protect their jobs. Family members, with very few exceptions, wanted the individual out of circulation, often for monetary gain. As a result, they all tended to desire a decision of 'insanity'.

This time, however, things would be different. Mr. Wingate Jones had been apprised of the fact that the gentleman, Mr. Norton, had nothing but support, and a great deal of it, except from the face-saving young officer who had placed him under arrest. Mr. Wingate Jones was prepared for the fact that the room would be wall to wall with friends and supporters of the accused. Oddly enough, he would have to count himself among their number. He was already convinced that Emperor Norton was not a lunatic, and that is what he had to explain to Chief Crowley.

It might also be prudent to note that Mr. Wingate Jones was ready to retire from his position as Commissioner of Lunacy, and this was certainly not the time for creating trouble where it wasn't needed. He was in the final stretch of his career and all he really wanted was smooth sailing from here on.

Shortly before eight o'clock, Chief Crowley arrived at his office. Mr. Wingate Jones, with great relief, followed him in like a shadow. Even before he had a chance to settle in, the Chief went to his desk, sat behind it, and gestured for Mr. Wingate Jones to occupy the chair opposite.

"I think I know what has you so agitated, Jones, and I am pretty sure my thoughts are about the same. Why don't you tell me what's on your mind."

"Absolutely, Chief Crowley. I'll get right to the point. I am not convinced that a public hearing to determine the soundness of mind of Joshua Norton is the right thing to do. In fact, I oppose such a move and believe it would not be in my best interest, your best interest, nor in the best interest of the City of San Francisco. It would be a useless exercise and would stir up so many hard feelings – and for what purpose? I can tell you right now that I don't believe he is insane. Nor is he in any way a danger to himself or to anyone else. In fact, his presence in this city has become a rather important asset to the business community. Even other cities have sent him gifts in hopes of luring him away from San Francisco. Certainly, you have seen the posters and placards in the restaurants and stores boldly proclaiming, 'By Appointment to His Majesty, Emperor Norton'. I am told he doesn't drink nor does he gamble, but he is still afforded the privilege of taking the free meals offered at various restaurants and saloons because of the goodwill it generates for those establishments."

Mr. Wingate Jones continued, "Surely you have passed merchants' stores selling Emperor Norton postcards and Emperor Norton dolls. Postcards and likenesses of him sell rather well, and many tourists even seek him out for his autograph. In addition, as one person pointed out to me last evening, he is officially (and I emphasize, officially) listed in the San Francisco Business Directory. If you look on page 372 you'll see it. It even gives his occupation as – you guessed it – Emperor. This man is considered of great benefit to the community and is a friend of many."

Chief Crowley nodded and said, "Thank you, Jones."

"Please let me finish, Chief Crowley. I have been going over this all night long and feel I have to have my say."

Mr. Wingate Jones' accident of birth had landed him on the

Zodiac chart in the house of Cancer. Like all Moon Children I know, he couldn't stop mid-stream in making his case. He had to finish his thoughts or they would clog up inside his head causing him great vexation, so he insisted that Chief Crowley let him continue.

"With all due respect sir, I must continue. It's important you understand this."

"Okay, then, Jones. Go ahead, I'm listening."

"As I said, Joshua Norton is a friend to many people. One would be hard pressed to find anyone who doesn't like him. Despite his position in life, he is still a very intelligent man. But after all is said and done, the most convincing argument I have is this: I had the opportunity to have a conversation with him one day a few months ago. During our talk, I made note of his delusion about being Emperor – to which he mounted a dignified protest. But then I asked him a very telling question. I asked if he ever thought he just might be insane, and he answered, 'Yes sir, I have – many times. And I believe the fact that I would even ask myself that question proves that I am, in fact, sane.' With that statement, even in the absence of all of the other details I have given you, I knew that he is, indeed, a sane man. As I think about it now, I sometimes think he just might be in more of a right mind than all the rest of us."

"Obviously, I need not ask what you think we should do," said Chief Crowley.

"No sir," said Mr. Wingate Jones. "I can't make it any plainer."

"Okay. I know that at ten o'clock there are going to be a lot of people arriving at the hearing room to attend the meeting. I'll meet them at the door and let them know that the hearing has been cancelled. It's all been a big mistake. Whatever. I'll come up with something good to say that will diffuse the situation and make them all happy. I mean, good God, this could have been a real cock-up. Thank you for your input. I couldn't have said it any better. You certainly have more insight than I do. So you don't worry. I'll take care of everything."

Less than two hours later, Chief Crowley went to the front doors of the city hall and in opening the door was met with a deafening howl from the large crowd of supporters that had gathered outside.

He attempted to quiet them and calm them down. "The meeting has been cancelled!" he shouted, and the people returned a roar of approval. Chief Crowley waved his arms up and down to silence the crowd. He waited patiently for the noise and agitation to subside.

"Please, let me make a statement to you, and listen carefully. When I finish you can hoot and holler all you want. On behalf of the San Francisco Police Department, I have offered Emperor Norton our official apology. A mistake was made, and we are doing what is necessary to improve our communication within the department. We do our best to look after the interests and the safety of the citizens of San Francisco even though our resources are often stretched beyond a reasonable limit. In this case we overstepped our bounds and have asked His Majesty to forgive us. He has graciously done so. It should not have come to this, and it certainly does not require a hearing to determine his mental state. There is no official reason to question his sanity, and statements from concerned citizens like all of you have proven that. It has also been sufficiently proven that he is recognized and appreciated as our Emperor. Therefore, from this day forward, I am instructing all police officers of the City of San Francisco to salute the Emperor whenever appropriate.

Again, everyone cheered in unanimous agreement. The entire crowd outside and down the street erupted into wild celebration.

Emperor Norton had heard Chief Crowley's statement from inside the building. Now the police will salute him. His mind went back many years to his childhood in Cape Town – to one of his few truly happy memories. He remembered how the sentries at the castle presented arms whenever Old Moses, the former soldier, approached. Like Old Moses, the Emperor was finally getting the respect he deserved. He came to the doorway and received the ovation his subjects lovingly sent his way. Waving and smiling, he placed his beaver hat atop his head and walked back to his Imperial Lodgings, his 6 x 9 room in a flophouse at 624 Commercial Street.

# CHAPTER 28

The issue was settled. Emperor Norton was not a vagrant, nor was he crazy. That was proven without the embarrassment of an official public hearing before the eminent Wingate Jones. Emperor Norton was who and what he claimed to be. He was pleased to have the validation of the people, of the city, and especially of the police department – in fact, of the Chief of Police, himself.

There was still a lingering doubt in his mind, and a bit of embarrassment, when he thought about being called a vagrant. That touched a nerve. It was true that he did not have a real, paying job, and it was true that he was depending on the kindness and goodwill of the people. The occasional gifts of small amounts of money were all he had. That's how he was able to have $4.75 in his pocket at the time of his arrest.

Relying on the generosity of others for his subsistence was something that had to end. He was sane, remember, and he was smart enough to know that referring to such gifts as "taxes" was a way to justify the gifts. It was dishonest, and he knew it.

It was true that certain restaurants and saloons benefited from offering him meals and from their association with him, so that wasn't a problem. It was the handouts that hurt his pride, so his entrepreneurial spirit kicked in once again. He was once a successful participant in the business world, so why not use some of that talent to become an enterprising Emperor? So he began to think of ways in which he could actively provide for himself.

The most realistic and practical solution, and one very much in keeping with his position, was for him to issue his own currency – notes which his subjects could purchase from him now, but for which there would be a maturity date sometime in the future when they would be repaid, with interest. That would provide an immediate benefit to his financial status, and would be an investment, by those individuals, in their future. It would be money earned as opposed to charity received, and his sense of honor would be preserved.

He began to speak with a few people about his plans. Most were encouraging to his face, but chuckled once his back was turned. One friend, however, was not only encouraging, but was also in a position to help him out.

Mr. Edward Hughes had been in San Francisco for about five years and, along with John Cuddy, had purchased a print shop from the "Two Toms", and renamed it "Cuddy and Hughes". Norton knew that Edward Hughes had apprenticed as a printer in Virginia City, Nevada, working for the Territorial Enterprise alongside a brilliant young writer – namely me.

Emperor Norton, using his entrepreneurial skills, knew that having something in common and a little name dropping went a long way in business dealings. So he chose a beautiful Spring morning to approach Mr. Hughes in his shop on Sansome Street.

"Good morning," said the Emperor as he entered through the front door. "I understand we have a friend in common."

"We do?" replied Mr. Hughes. "Of whom do you speak?" To Norton's ear, that "whom" identified Mr. Edward Hughes as a well-educated man.

"Mr. Samuel Clemens! He has been a friend of mine ever since his time in San Francisco, and I understand you worked with him up in Virginia City."

"Oh, yes indeed. A talented young man. He seems to be making quite a name for himself!"

"Yes," said the Emperor, "he is making a name for himself – Mark Twain!"

They both laughed.

"I mean he is becoming a shining star in his chosen field as a writer and speaker," said Mr. Hughes.

"That he has."

"What can I do for you?" asked Mr. Hughes.

"Well, sir, as Emperor of the United States, I have decided that I need to issue my own currency – in the form of notes. I plan to call them 'Bonds of the Empire'. My intention is to sell some for their face value now, payable with interest at a later date, and to use others as payment for services rendered – also redeemable to the holder in the future.

Edward Hughes took a liking to Emperor Norton, and admired the organized manner in which he presented his idea. It was obvious he had thoroughly considered all aspects.

"And what's in it for me?" asked Hughes.

"Well, sir, I am embarrassed to say that I cannot afford to pay you for your services. However, I think it would be beneficial to you if the notes were designed to carry your imprint at the bottom of each note. Everyone will know that these Bonds of the Empire were printed by Cuddy and Hughes, they will be informed of your address, they will see the quality of your work, and they will be impressed by the fact that you are printers by appointment to, well, me, their beloved Emperor! If anything was a winning proposition, it is this."

Hughes was impressed by the Emperor and by his idea. A deal

was struck. Cuddy and Hughes would design and print Bonds of the Empire in 50-cent and $5.00 denominations. They would offer a seven per-cent interest rate and would be payable in 1880. At the bottom would appear the following: "Cuddy and Hughes, Printers to His Majesty Norton I, 511 Sansome Street, S.F."

Cuddy and Hughes were already printing picture postcards of Emperor Norton for another company, which were being sold to the tourist trade. With several likenesses of the Emperor to choose from, the notes were designed to feature a small portrait of him. Early versions were dated, and were worded in the form of a receipt. "Received of (name of purchaser), Fifty Cents. The amount with interest to be convertible into seven percent bonds in 1880 as payable by the agents of our Private Estate in case the government of Norton the First does not hold firm." There were then spaces for the Emperor's signature and the date issued.

Norton soon realized there were a couple problems with this version. In the form of a receipt, it narrowed the purposes for which the notes could be used. What if, for example, he wanted to use them as payment for services rendered? He also didn't like the reference to the possibility that his government would not "hold firm". That showed a sign of weakness. So the notes were reworded and made even more professional. They read: "The Imperial Government of Norton I promises to pay the holder hereof, the sum of Fifty Cents in the year 1880 at 7 percent, per annum from date; the principal and interest to be convertible, at the option of the holder, at maturity, into 20 years 7 percent bonds or payable in Gold Coin." Norton also liked the idea of giving the holder the option to trade it for another note, rather than to cash it in. He could sign and date the notes. In order to heighten the official status of these notes, the Emperor decided he would also ink his fingerprint onto each note, or, to form a seal, he would ink up a coin and press it onto the paper.

Mr. Hughes, having access to other illustrations, decided on an updated design. He would add a female figure to the note in the opposite corner from the Emperor's portrait. This, unfortunately, happened at a time when Emperor Norton had expressed an interest in finding a woman to become his Empress. People teased him about this – to the point that he became rather embarrassed and angry about the situation. As a result, the Emperor withdrew all of the offending notes from circulation and fired Cuddy and Hughes. They were no longer going to be his royal printers.

It was well known that Emperor Norton tended to favor the Unitarian Church for his Sunday worship. There, he had befriended Mr. Charles Murdock, a printer, who had traveled a great deal and had been involved in many different business ventures that Emperor Norton enjoyed talking with him about.

Emperor Norton presented a plan to Mr. Murdock, proposing that he become the new printer of the royal warrant. Murdock was impressed with his seriousness, his determination, and had seen the success of his earlier Bonds of the Empire. The clincher, though, was when the Emperor said: "When I come into my true estate, I will make you Chancellor of the Exchequer!" How could he say no? This time, Norton wanted notes in the denominations of 50 cents and ten dollars; with the greatest number to be printed in the 50-cent denomination. Obviously, that was the most popular investment! This time, the woman would be replaced with an official seal. Further, it was decided that, in a money-saving move, the interest rate would be lowered from 7 percent to 5 percent.

The woman was gone from Emperor Norton's currency, but not from his mind. Mr. Murdock was not only his printer, but also a friend, and was quite influential within the community of the Unitarian Church. So the Emperor asked him to keep his eyes open as perhaps he could select a suitable Empress from among the ladies of the church. But second thoughts set in, as Norton was not a man to subject his Empress to a squalid room in a boarding house. So the printing job was on, but the search for a lady was cancelled.

He said to Mr. Murdock, "No man ever thought of keeping a bird until he had a cage, and a queen must have a palace."

# CHAPTER 29

Two of Emperor Norton's friends, with whom he spent many a day in conversation, were engineers. This is not unusual, as the Emperor had a great mind for engineering and scientific endeavors.

Frederick Marriott had come to San Francisco in the late '40's to seek his fortune. A successful newspaperman in his native England, he helped finance and publicize what turned out to be an unsuccessful fixed-wing airplane flight (it was he who coined the word "aeroplane"). He came to California with the idea of making a fortune in the gold fields, but, like Norton, Robertson, Lick, and others, he found it wiser to earn his fortune in more secure ways. He opened a bank and succeeded in selling real estate loans. Then, building upon his newspaper experience in England, he founded the *San Francisco News Letter*, along with several other publications. The *News Letter* was unique in that it consisted of a blue sheet of paper with news articles on one side, and a blank page on the other, "letter", side, allowing San Franciscans to send hard news as well as correspondence to their far-flung relatives. It, too, was a big success.

With his profits from these ventures, Marriott founded the Aerial Steam Navigation Company with the intention of building a lighter-than-air flying balloon. Emperor Norton supported his efforts and loved to discuss the details of its development.

Andrew Hallidie, Norton's other friend, was of Scottish descent and hailed from England. Hallidie came to California in the early '50's with the idea of developing aerial cableways for use in the gold fields – in order to transport equipment and supplies across rivers and rough terrain. They developed the manufacture and use of wire ropes which were strong enough to carry heavy loads. Needless to say, they were extremely successful.

While in the midst of building his ropeways in the gold fields, Andrew Hallidie couldn't help but dwell on the great need for some type of railway transportation in the City of San Francisco. While aerial ropeways would not be practical, he thought that a similar type of continuous cable at ground level might work. In the late '60's, Hallidie devoted a lot of time exploring these possibilities in the city, and spent many hours researching and discussing his ideas at the Mechanics' Institute.

One late morning in June of 1869 found Emperor Norton in the library of the Mechanics' Institute having a pleasant conversation with Frederick Marriott. Marriott was on the verge of testing his flying balloon and had much to say about its status. Suddenly, there was a commotion out in the main lobby. The entrance door had slammed shut, and heavy footsteps pounded the floor.

From within the library, Norton and Marriott heard a short exchange between Hallidie and Mr. Beldon Shaw, the club butler at the Mechanics' Institute. Seconds later, Hallidie burst through the door of the library and went straight to a chair opposite the two gentlemen.

"I know I'm very late, gentlemen, but I just witnessed the most god-awful accident I have ever seen. Forgive me, I'm a bit shaken up. I don't usually have a drink before lunchtime."

"Since when?" muttered Norton, under his breath.

"I beg your pardon?" asked Hallidie, mildly upset that he was interrupted mid-statement.

"I am sorry, but I did not hear what you said," he lied.

"Get a horn, Norton!" He paused and quieted himself. "Forgive me – again – but as I said, I am rather shaken up. I have asked Shaw to bring me three fingers of scotch to calm my nerves."

"Tell us about the accident," said Marriott.

"Oh, my goodness, it was tragic. I was walking past Powell Street early this morning. Wet and windy it was. A heavy delivery cart, pulled by four horses, was struggling to get up the hill and suddenly one of the horses slipped on the wet cobblestones and lost his footing."

Shaw entered at that moment with Hallidie's scotch.

"Oh, thank you Shaw. I really need this." He downed a generous swallow.

"The poor creature fell and, in doing so, knocked over one of the other horses. The remaining two horses didn't have the strength to hold it and the entire cart began slipping backwards down the hill. The poor fool driving the cart pulled on his brake, but the damn chain snapped and he lost all control."

"Good grief!" gasped Norton.

"So, what happened?" asked Marriott, frowning and leaning intently forward.

Hallidie continued: "The cart and all its heavy load jerked backwards and quickly increased its speed, careening down the hill. The remaining two horses then lost their footing and fell, and the driver appeared frozen, choosing to remain aboard rather than jump off.

"When the cart reached the bottom of the hill, it tipped over, throwing its contents, including the driver, out across the road. The poor horses, in agony, lay there in a pile of bloodied flesh and broken bones. The driver was dead, having struck his head when he was thrown from the cart."

"What about the horses?" asked Norton.

"They were so badly injured – each and every one – beyond hope. Some avenging angel went and found a gun and in four shots finished off the poor, suffering animals."

Hallidie took a second large swig of scotch, finishing it off.

"I saw something similar a while back," said Marriott. "It was a small cart with about a dozen people aboard. They, however, were going down a rather steep hill when the horse lost his footing. The people were fine, but the cart ran partially over the horse, pushing him down the hill underneath the front wheels. He didn't have to be shot, though, as he was dead by the time they stopped."

"In all my time inspecting the streets around the city," said Emperor Norton, "I have never witnessed such horrible things. The odd horse loses its footing and slips, yes, but never with tragic results as these of which you speak. The last such tragedies I remember were years ago when the streets were all dirt and sand, and occasionally, after a rainstorm, the poor horses became mired in the mud and were left to die."

"Well, I can tell you," said Hallidie, "this incident has given me increased motivation to get some sort of cable-driven transportation to negotiate these damnable hills, and let the horses do other, safer jobs. I'm going to work hard on that, and if it proves to be financially sound, I'll see that it gets completed."

# CHAPTER 30

I had great admiration for Frederick Marriott. I worked for him for a short time, writing articles for his *News Letter* and his *California Advertiser*.

I spent many evenings down in his basement watching him work on his project. Having only the light of candles stuck into empty beer bottles, he diligently poured over his plans and created what he called his "Hermes Avitor". I was impressed with his diligence and his constant enthusiasm.

His final design consisted of a large gas-filled balloon in the shape of a very fat cigar. It was 37 feet long, and 14 feet wide. It was powered by a steam engine, driving two propellers mounted on flat wings which protruded from the sides. He found in his testing that the balloon took about six minutes to fill with hydrogen.

Mr. Marriott's work paid off. On the morning of July 2, 1869, he and his shareholders and eager supporters, including Emperor

Norton, rose early and took the railway down the Bay to the south of the city. They went by buggy from the station to Shell Mound Park where the Avitor works were located. The "Hermes Avitor" floated out of the building. Two men, standing fore and aft held ropes in order to prevent the craft from floating away and ran around the park while the hydrogen kept it aloft and the propellers moved it along. The airship flew at about five miles per hour, making two complete half-mile circles around the park.

By that time I had moved along, but in a letter to the Alta California newspaper, I had begged, *Send us more news about Mr. Marriott's air-ship … It is a subject that is bound to stir the pulses of any man, for in this age of inventive wonders, all men have come to believe that in some genius' brain sleeps the solution of the grand problem of aerial navigation – and along with that belief is the hope that that genius will reveal his miracle before they die, and likewise a dread that he will poke off somewhere and die himself before he finds out that he has such a wonder lying dormant in his brain. We all know that air can be navigated – therefore hurry up your sails and bladders – satisfy us – let us have peace … Tell us about the Avitor. We wish to hear that it is a success.*

Of course, I precociously added the comment that with railroads, steamers, the ocean telegraph, and the air ship finally secured, we only have one single wonder left to work at, and that is telegraphic communion with the people of Jupiter and the Moon! *I am dying to see some of those fellows*, I had said.

As I have indicated, Emperor Norton was also a great supporter of Mr. Marriott's endeavors and following the flight of the "Hermes Avitor", he issued one of his famous proclamations:

> *Whereas, we, Norton I, 'Dei Gratia' Emperor of the United States, being anxious for the future fame and honor of the residents of San Francisco, do hereby command all our good and loyal subjects to furnish the means and exert their best skill and advance money to make Mr. Marriott's aerial machine a success.*

Only later did Marriott determine that such steam-powered, lighter-than-air flight was not feasible. He moved on to the idea of heavier-than-air flight, but has not realized his dream.

Andrew Hallidie, on the other hand, has achieved great success. He was moved by the accidents he had seen, where horses and humans had suffered on the steep hills, and was motivated to do something about it. But it had to be feasible, practical, and economically sound. By '71, he knew how it could be done, so he constructed and patented a model of his cable-driven car. Funding was forthcoming, and he was able to lay a cable in an underground conduit, propelled by machinery at a fixed station. Grips took a long time to perfect, so that the cable car could safely attach to the constantly-moving cable, and disengage in order to come to a stop.

On August 1, 1873, early in the morning, Andrew Hallidie, along with his crew and supporters, stood at the top of the hill at the intersection of Clay and Leavenworth. Shrouded in fog, nearly 500 feet below, the end of the line seemed so very far away. The gentleman chosen to make the first run had a last-minute change of heart (and a loss of backbone), and refused to take the car down the hill. So Hallidie took his place, grabbed the grip, and safely took his car down the hill and into the fog at Kearny Street. Then the car was turned around on a turntable built specifically for that purpose and Hallidie gripped the cable and took the car all the way back up to the top. In less than a week, passengers were riding the cable cars up and down the hill. This new invention was a success, and eventually other hills of the city were challenged and conquered.

First, however, according to the Emperor, it had to pass his personal inspection. He determined that there were two items he considered "dangerous to the lives of the passengers." This prototype of the cable car was actually two small cars hooked together. The "dummy" car carried the driver and the gripping system. It consisted of a wheel connected to a large screw operating the grip which grabbed onto the moving cable. This "dummy" car was also designed to hold about eight passengers. The second car was designed to accommodate a dozen more. Emperor Norton concluded that this was a dangerous design and that there should only be one car. The second detail troubling him was the weakness of that large screw. He felt it was prone to fail.

Andrew Hallidie proceeded in spite of the Emperor's warnings. While he wouldn't admit it publicly, Hallidie eventually realized there was, indeed, a problem with the screw and changed it, eliminating the wheel and screw in favor of a lever system to grip the cable. To this day, the two-car design has not been altered, but I understand they are considering doing some tests with one double-ended car.

Of course, Emperor Norton won't get any credit for being proven right. If he were alive today, he would just shrug his shoulders and carry on.

# CHAPTER 31

On one tragic day, two trains of the transcontinental railroad were involved in a head-on collision due to a switchman's faulty timepiece. Shortly thereafter, Ambrose Bierce, a young writer and satirist for Frederick Marriott's *San Francisco News Letter,* saw a notice posted in an Oakland railroad station. It drew his interest and curiosity:

> *Hereafter, when two trains moving in opposite directions are approaching each other on separate tracks, conductors and engineers will be required to bring their respective trains to a dead halt before the point of meeting, and will be very careful not to proceed until each train has passed the other.*

How, he asked in one of his columns, could two trains pass each other while both are at a "dead halt"?

Bierce's mention of that notice, and his satirical perplexity over the wording of said notice, piqued Emperor Norton's curiosity and stimulated his grey cells. In fairly short order he came up with a brilliant solution – a switch that worked automatically. His discovery was announced in a very respected journal, *The Mining and Scientific Press*, and was read by his fellow members of the Mechanics' Institute:

> *Emperor Norton has invented a Railroad Switch, a model of which is now being made. It consists of a novel application of a spiral or elliptical spring, operated by the weight of the passing train, by which the Switch is turned off or on as desired. Patent applied for.*

Emperor Norton was delighted. He was now truly in the company of men he respected so greatly: Frederick Marriott, with his lighter-than-air flying machine; Andrew Hallidie, who, with his father, held patents on wire ropes and suspension bridges; and even President Abraham Lincoln, rest his soul, who once held a patent for a machine which would raise grounded ships off the shoals.

However, Norton's hopes were dashed. Asking Andrew Hallidie to make his switch model, he was told it would cost him $100. So the Emperor wrote a draft for that amount and took it to the First National Bank, whereupon it was refused.

Norton was angry. Rushing to the library of the Mechanics' Institute, he grabbed some stationery and wrote the following proclamation:

> ***WHEREAS***, *the First National Bank refused to honor a small check of $100, to pay the value of a model for a Railway Switch invented by us, thereby endangering our private interest to a large estate:*

**AND, WHEREAS**, *it is publicly notorious that one or two of the Directors have large amounts in trust belonging to our personal estate;*

**NOW, THEREFORE**, *we, Norton I, Emperor of the United States and Protector of Mexico, do hereby decree the confiscation to the State of all interest of said Bank as security for any losses we may sustain by reason of their acts.*

Of course, Norton's response did no good. The model was never made. The patent was never applied for. A pinch-penny friend and a recalcitrant banker prevented Norton's switch from ever being made – much to the loss of the railroad and its passengers.

There is one idea of Emperor Norton's, however, that was acted upon, which greatly enhanced the lives of the people and the economy of the town of Petaluma. Located north of San Francisco, across the bay, Petaluma was limited in its ability to conduct commerce with other cities in the Bay Area due to its extremely crooked creek which meandered down to San Francisco Bay in a series of S-shaped turns. These turns were shallow and plagued with silt that collected at every bend. As a result, commercial cargo could not be carried up or down the creek. Even passenger steamers, such as the *Gold*, could only go part way up the creek. Passengers had to disembark and transfer to stage coaches in order to travel the last seven miles to Petaluma. Needless to say, commerce was equally hindered, with cargoes having to go in smaller amounts by more difficult and time-consuming methods.

Norton gave great thought to the problem and came up with a very simple idea.

"Why do you not just straighten out the river?"

By golly, he had something there. They could dredge a straight line through, avoiding each and every S-curve, thus allowing the silt to flow into the bay, the water to be deeper, and shipping able to navigate the entire length from Petaluma to San Francisco Bay.

If you were able to fly over this area in one of Mr. Marriott's aeroplanes, you would see the lazy curves of the river slashed through with Emperor Norton's straight, deep, navigable channel.

Of course, Petaluma's love affair with Emperor Norton was greatly enhanced. The people of this far province of his empire provided their services to him with great generosity.

# CHAPTER 32

Emperor Norton's later years, during the bulk of the 1870's, were basically happy times. He was enjoying the fruits of having established his empire in the hearts of the people of San Francisco, and in the increasing numbers of visitors and tourists who sought him out for conversation and autographs. The City of San Francisco had grown and matured to the point where his daily peregrinations, inspecting and correcting, were not needed. While he still looked out for the best interests of his people, the Emperor took more time for himself. Reading. Conversation. Chess games. Theatre. Debates. Speeches.

Local newspaper wags spent a lot of time mocking him and libeling him in what they thought were humorous ways – attributing to him proclamations he never wrote. It was also a common practice to publish false telegrams purportedly received by the Emperor from Queen Victoria and other kings and queens of Europe. Albert Evans – known publicly as Colonel Moustache because of the long, waxed facial hair that protruded from his upper lip – wrote for several newspapers, using various pen names. He was relentless in satirizing the Emperor and writing false proclamations, greatly aggravating His Royal Personage. Oddly, they were easy to spot as none of them were written with the intelligence or style of the original. In spite of this, Emperor Norton had had enough:

> ***WHEREAS***, *there is every now and then a street report that the Emperor has received a telegram, or that he has done so and so, and on investigation found to be without foundation or fact;*
>
> ***WHEREAS***, *we are anxious that there should be no deception, and also that no imposter should make use of our authority;*
>
> ***KNOW, THEREFORE***, *all whom it may concern that no act is legal unless it has our imperial signature.*
>
> *Signed, Norton the First, Emperor of the United States*

The Emperor did continue writing proclamations on issues of great importance. Two of his proclamations generated great interest. The most compelling of these proclamations, issued in 1872, was the one which reflected his conviction that San Francisco and the East Bay should be connected by a bridge:

> *The following is decreed and ordered to be carried into execution as soon as convenient: 1. That a suspension bridge be built from Oakland Point to Goat Island and thence to Telegraph Hill; provided such bridge can be built without injury to navigable waters of the Bay of San Francisco. 2. That the Central Pacific*

> *Railroad Company be granted franchises to lay down tracks and run cars from Telegraph Hill and along the city front to Mission Bay.*

Perhaps one day, with the growth of these cities, Emperor Norton's bridge will become a reality.

Another decree had to do with the identification of San Francisco as "Frisco", as it appeared on the markings of the Central Pacific Railroad. Emperor Norton felt that "Frisco" was an inappropriate way to identify or refer to the city named for St. Francis. To this effect, he issued a proclamation:

> *Whoever after due and proper warning shall be heard to utter the abominable word, "Frisco", which has no linguistic or other warrant, shall be deemed guilty of a High Misdemeanor, and shall pay into the Imperial Treasury as penalty the sum of twenty-five dollars.*

This proclamation is still diligently observed by the loyal citizenry of San Francisco.

There was a personal issue that Emperor Norton visited for one last time. He still thought often about his lack of an Empress. He had once issued a proclamation generally seeking housing fit for a royal family:

> *WHEREAS, our friends and adherent are dissatisfied that we are not better lodged, and hold that we ought to have had a suitable palace years ago;*
>
> *WHEREAS, the treasonable proscriptive acts of some of the hotel keepers of this city have kept us out of decent rooms for our accommodations, so that we have been unable to make our family arrangements in order.*

*NOW, THEREFORE, we do hereby command the proprietors of the Grand Hotel to forthwith furnish us with rooms, under penalty of being banished.*

The royal abode was not forthcoming – nor was anyone banished.

In the meantime, Emperor Norton had fallen in love – at a distance – with the young, 17-year-old, daughter of a former sea captain. Her name was Minnie Wakeman.

Emperor Norton was uncharacteristically ebullient. In anticipation of this future Empress, he avidly sought appropriate lodgings and wrote a new proclamation:

*WHEREAS, it is our intention to take an Empress, and in consideration of the visits by the Royalty abroad, we, Norton I, Dei Gratia Emperor of the United States and Protector of Mexico, do hereby command the builders of the Palace Hotel to fit up a portion of their building for our Imperial Residence, as becoming the dignity of a great and hopeful nation.*

He then wrote to his intended:

*My dear Miss Wakeman:*

*In arranging for my Empress, I shall be delighted if you will permit me to make use of your name. Should you be willing, please let me know but keep your own secret. It is a safer way I think.*

*Your Devoted loving friend, The Emperor*

When he tried to visit at her home, he was rebuffed. He later received a lovely note from her declining his invitation, and indicating that she was already promised to another man. Cut to the quick, he responded:

*My dear Miss Minnie:*

*I did not receive your note until this morning, having been absent nearly a fortnight attending the Legislature. Otherwise would not have been so rude as to call on you yesterday. Regret extremely your previous engagement. Hope is if anything should occur to break it off, you will think of one who loves you to distraction.*

*The State expects me to get my Lady and travel to Washington and I must look to the Ladies to answer.*

*Yours faithfully, Norton I*

Emperor Norton never did find a woman to share his palace and his life. He finally accepted the fact that he was alone, and accepted what he came to think of as his predestined single life – ruling over his people without the companionship he had desired.

One of the highlights of the Emperor's later life occurred in 1876, when Dom Pedro II, the Emperor of Brazil, came to San Francisco on an official visit. Dom Pedro specifically requested a meeting with the Emperor of the United States. Norton was overjoyed.

He spent extra time beating the dust out of his official jacket. He made sure his epaulets were straight and as shiny as possible. He dusted his hat and straightened the feather. And of course his walking stick, his closed Chinese umbrella, and his royal saber finished the uniform.

The two emperors met for more than an hour in a royal suite at the newly-opened Palace Hotel (a far cry from the original Palace Hotel where Emperor Norton was arrested so many years before). They talked politics, history, literature, science, and their hopes for the future.

Dom Pedro never revealed whether or not he realized that the Emperor of the United States was not the real thing. Odds are, he didn't.

The Emperor plodded on, having survived his previous life as a successful businessman, his wilderness years after his fall, and his life as a monarch, with its trials and its triumphs. He was, indeed, a survivor.

James Lick, his original landlord, died in 1876 – an extremely wealthy man. Lick left an estate of more than $3 million. Through the years he had promoted the development of San Francisco and had invested greatly in city real estate and country real estate. Even though he had built one of the most luxurious hotels in San Francisco, the eponymous Lick House, he continued to deny himself and lived as though a pauper. Although he earned the reputation of being a miser, he was generous to others. His estate, based upon his express desires, was used, among other things, to build a school of mechanical arts, to fund orphanages, to build an old ladies' home, and to build the largest telescope in the world.

The scoundrel, "Honest" Harry Meiggs, died in 1877. Once he and his family sailed out of San Francisco Bay, back in 1852, they headed all the way to Tahiti. Following a nice vacation there, they sailed back to Chile where he succeeded, beyond his dreams, building railroads. Meiggs had a change of heart, becoming a well-liked and trusted man. He decided he wanted to return to San Francisco, and with his newly-made fortune, paid back all the money he had stolen from the city. Friends back home – yes, he still had a few – wanted to have all charges against him dropped (It is interesting to note that at that time, embezzlement was not a felony). His friends persuaded both houses of the California Legislature to pass a bill pardoning him of his crimes. In the end, the governor would not sign it. "Honest" Harry never came home. He died in Lima, Peru – a very rich and famous man.

Sam Brannan, ever the entrepreneur, bought land in the Napa Valley, built a resort, and founded the town of Calistoga (deftly combining the words "California" and the fashionable "Saratoga"

Springs, New York). He also founded the Napa Valley Railroad, making it easy for tourists to visit his resort. The railroad was, perhaps, his one failure. It was sold at a foreclosure sale in 1869.

Then, in 1872, his wife divorced him. It was ruled that he had to give her half of his fortune, payable in cash. Since much of his wealth was in real estate, he had to liquidate most of his properties in order to pay her off.

Domingo Ghirardelli is still alive, in 1880, and continues to make the best chocolate in San Francisco. He has diversified his business to include, besides his world-class chocolate, coffee and spices, which he sells across the United States, Mexico, China and Japan.

Frederick Marriott has ended his efforts to fly. His lighter-than-air experiments died with the stock market crash in 1869, and later efforts with heavier-than-air machines were fruitless.

Andrew Hallidie served as President of the San Francisco Mechanics' Institute and remains active in numerous scientific societies. He ran unsuccessfully for the California State Senate in 1873, and ran, again unsuccessfully, for Mayor of San Francisco in 1875. He is now, as of 1880, a regent of the University of California. His patents on his cable car design have made him a very wealthy man.

Peter Robertson, after he returned to Baltimore, never again communicated with the Emperor.

# CHAPTER 33

January 7, 1880. Evening. This was the time of year when days were short and nights were long. Emperor Norton spent an average day making his rounds and looked forward to another usual day tomorrow. He would get up at about seven, dress in his uniform coat with the tarnished brass buttons and golden epaulets, and his old boots. He would pick up his grapevine walking stick and, if it was raining, his Chinese umbrella. He would pick up his tall beaver hat with the rosette and ostrich feather, and carry it under his left arm – to be placed on his head once he steps out the door. Norton would stop downstairs to pay his daily rent, and then walk next door to read newspapers at the Empire Hotel.

The Emperor then would stop for breakfast (free, of course) at one of the local restaurants. More often than not, he would forgo a walking tour, electing instead to visit a school (he loved the young children) or to head directly to Portsmouth Square for conversation.

The Emperor was older now, in his early sixties, and life had taken its toll. He tired more easily. He walked more slowly, and the corns on his feet were worse than ever. It had been necessary for him to cut even larger slits in his boots in order to accommodate them. He reflected philosophically on the fact that he was still alive and able to rule over his country and his city. Through the last 40 years he had known so many people who died – starting with his entire family. On the way to San Francisco he knew several passengers who had died of scurvy and other ailments. In the early days he knew people who died from rat bites, and from violence brought on by the Hounds or the Sydney Ducks, or various other hoodlums who ran wild for a time. He knew people who had died in the fires that engulfed the young city, and who drowned in the bay on countless stormy days. He knew people who died in San Francisco's recent bout with cholera. By the grace of God, he was still here.

In these later days, Emperor Norton retired early, lit the lamp in his room, and read. During the days he would spend at the Mechanics' Library, or the Bohemian Club, he would read the news and articles on science or history. In the evenings, he liked classics like the *Iliad* or *Odyssey* from Homer, or *Pilgrim's Progress*, or a Shakespeare play, or, his favorite, *Don Quixote* by Miguel de Cervantes.

Tomorrow evening, though, he was going to attend a lecture put on by the Hastings Society at the Academy of Sciences. He was certain that, as usual, they would ask him to say a few words prior to the beginning of the debate. He used to do this sort of thing extemporaneously, but now felt more comfortable planning what he might say, even writing it down to assist his failing memory. For the following evening, he wanted to say a few words reflecting on his time as Emperor and the debt he owed to the people of the city – much more so than any debt they would owe him, aside from the usual respect. He was thankful for the time they have allowed him to rule over them.

# CHAPTER 34

The Emperor never made it to the Academy of Sciences on the evening of January 8. He keeled over and died before help could arrive. As he fell, his beloved beaver hat, its ostrich feather standing atop, fell onto the wet street, where the once-proud plume wilted in the rain-soaked gutter.

Emperor Norton left behind no heirs. His worldly goods, mostly found in his pockets, amounted to a $2.50 gold piece, $3.00 in silver, a French Franc dated 1828, and a stock certificate for over 1,000,000 shares in a worthless gold mine. The French Franc was the very one that Peter Robertson had given him, back in the salad days of long ago. It had never left his pocket. Also found in his tiny lodgings was a small collection of walking sticks (gifts from various cities, recognizing the publicity he created, vying to win him away from San Francisco), and his tasseled saber, which he had elected to leave at home on that fateful night.

The City of San Francisco went into mourning. Ten thousand people lined up at the undertaking establishment at #16 O'Farrell Street to view his remains. His body was clothed in a black robe with a white shirt and black tie. Countless mourners barely recognized him without his dirty army uniform. Visitors to his viewing included the gamut of humanity, from wealthy bankers to pickpockets, from clergymen and society ladies to some of the lowest members of society.

One particularly well dressed lady brought a boutonniere of tuberose and maiden's hair, asking politely if she might place it upon his lapel.

"I have known Mr. Norton from the time I was a very young girl," she said. "He was very successful back then, and was always very kind to me. Even after the onset of his delusion, I have seen him many times. He never lost his fine manners nor his courtesy. Although he thought himself an emperor, I always thought he was a prince of a man."

Looking back upon his life, I have to agree with that young lady. He was every bit a prince. A king. Nay, an emperor!

On the day of his funeral, over 30,000 people lined the two-mile route followed by his funeral cortege on its way to the Masonic Cemetery. Flags were flown at half-mast, businesses closed, and people gathered to pay their last respects and then organized a large, exuberant street party that lasted for several days.

As you probably know, I came into this world with Halley's Comet, and it's due back in our celestial neighborhood in about 25 more years. I've always said I will also go out with Halley's Comet. The verity of that remains to be seen. Emperor Norton went out with, perhaps, an even more impressive planetary show of power. Not only did the City of San Francisco go into mourning at his passing – so did the entire solar system. As he was lowered into the ground, at 2:39 p.m., there was an eclipse of the sun. Need I say that I am filled with a feeling of jealousy?

On a final note, there was one more item found in the Emperor's pocket when they laid him out at the undertaker's. They found the paper with his notes to be used for his short speech at the hall on that fateful evening. His notes revealed what I would consider an uncanny moment of clarity and understanding, belying any delusion of which he might be accused. Emperor Norton – Joshua Norton – gave a very strong indication that perhaps the joke was really on us. In his written notes, which he had prepared for the following evening's comments, he quoted a scene from Shakespeare's *King Henry the 6ᵗʰ – Part 3*. I let it speak for itself:

> *King Henry has entered, disguised, carrying a prayer book. After some conversation, the Gamekeeper says: "Say, what art thou talk'st of kings and queens?*
>
> *King Henry: More than I seem, and less than I was born to; A man at least, for less I should not be; And men may talk of kings, and why not I?*
>
> *Gamekeeper: Ay, but thou talk'st as if thou wert a king.*
>
> *King Henry: Why, so I am – in mind, and that's enough.*
>
> *Gamekeeper: But if thou be a king, where is thy crown?*
>
> *King Henry: My crown is in my heart, not on my head; Not deck'd with diamonds and Indian stones, Nor to be seen. My crown is call'd content, A crown it is that seldom kings enjoy.*

CPSIA information can be obtained at www.ICGtesting.com
Printed in the USA
BVOW08*1330290315

393692BV00001B/1/P